DISKAN SHIVERED. Of what could he be sure? Never before had he been forced to look outside himself and guess what was real and what was not; he had been only too well aware of the real. He had traveled with the furred ones in both the real and the unreal, so how could he be sure of either anymore? Perhaps today was also a dream—perhaps Diskan Fentress lay encased in the mud-filled spacer. He jerked away from that path of thought. No—for the second time he stamped. *This* was real! This was now and it was real. And, judging by those tracks, another of his kind had found it real before him.

What was about to happen? This expectancy was a part of it all, a waiting, growing intensity, willing him to do something, be somewhere. . . .

THE X FACTOR

Andre Norton

FAWCETT CREST • NEW YORK

THE X FACTOR

Published by Fawcett Crest Books, a unit of CBS Publications, the Consumer Publishing Division of CBS Inc., by arrangement with Harcourt Brace Jovanovich, Inc.

ISBN: 0-449-24395-8

Printed in the United States of America

First Fawcett Crest Printing: April 1981

10   9   8   7   6   5   4   3   2   1

For Helen Hoover,
whose weasel-fisher people
gave me the Brothers-in-Fur

ONE

Even nighttime on Vaanchard was disturbing. It was not a time of peace in which one could hide. There were gemlike glints in the garden path, a soft luminescence to the growing things, new scents and—

Diskan Fentress hunched over, his chin almost touching his knees, fingertips thrust into his ears. He had closed his eyes to his surroundings, too—though there was no way to filter those scents out of the air he breathed. His mouth worked; he was afraid he was going to be thoroughly and disastrously sick, right here where his shame would be public. Not that anyone would let him see their disgust, of course. The elaborate pretense that Diskan Fentress was one of them would continue and continue and continue—He swallowed convulsively.

The greenish moonlight had reached the edge of the path now, awaking the glints to crystalline brilliance. A new fragrance tantalized his nostrils, but not aggressively. Diskan could not imagine anything in this garden as aggressive. When created and brought to perfection by the Vaans, a pleasure place was subtle.

Diskan fought a silent struggle against his heaving insides, against the terrible bonds this garden and the building from which he had fled, this city, this world, had laid upon him. His trouble reached back farther

7

than just his coming here to Vaanchard—to a day when Ulken the Overseer had brought a stranger down to the pond back on Nyborg, had called Diskan out from the murky water, where he stood up to his middle, green slime smearing his bare body, and had spoken to him as if he were a—a *thing*—not a man with feelings and a mind, if not a body, like his fellows.

Now Diskan's breath came in a ragged sob. His eyes might register the path and the strange growth, if he wanted to look, all the elfin glory of the night, but *he* saw the past now.

His troubles had not begun by the pond either, but back down the trail of years. His mouth shaped a grimace, half a snarl of frustrated rage. Way back, that beginning—

He could not remember any time when he had not been aware of the truth, that Diskan Fentress was a reject—a badly working piece of human machinery that could be turned only to the simplest and dirtiest of jobs. He did not know how to use the outsize share of strength in his poorly coordinated body, breaking when he wanted to mend or cherish. And his mind functioned almost as badly—slowly and stupidly.

Why? How many times had he demanded that in the past, ever since he could think and wonder at all! But he had learned quickly not to ask it of anyone but himself—and that impersonal power that might or might not have had a hand in his misfashioning.

Back on Nyborg he had—would they say—"adjusted"? At least being used for the brute-strength jobs left him mostly to himself during the day, and that was escape of a kind, something he did not have here.

Then, in spite of shrinking from that memory, Diskan thought again of the scene by the pond. Ulken, filthy, coarse, but still judged infinitely higher in the community scale than Diskan, standing there, a sly grin on his face, shouting as if his victim were deaf in addition to all the rest.

And the man with him—Diskan closed his eyes,

8

licked his lips before he swallowed again, willing himself not to—no, no!

That man, lithe, of middle height, all feline grace and ease, his fine body well displayed in the brown-green uniform of Survey, the silver comet of a First-in Scout on his breast! The stranger had looked so clean, so close to the ideal of Diskan's haunted dreams that he had simply stared at him, not answering Ulken's shouted orders—until he saw that *blackness* on the Scout's face, just before the Scout had turned on Ulken. The overseer had shriveled and backed off. But when the Scout had looked at Disken once more, Ulken had grinned, maliciously, before he slouched away.

"You are—Diskan Fentress?" Disbelief, yes, there had been disbelief in that, enough to awaken in Diskan some of the old defiance.

He had waded out of the water, pulling up fistfuls of coarse grass to rub the slime from him.

"I'm Fentress."

"So am I. Renfry Fentress."

Diskan had not really understood, not for a whole moment of suspended time. He had gone right on wiping his big clumsy body. Then he answered with the truth as he had known it.

"But you're dead!"

"There's sometimes a light-year stretch between presumption and actuality," the Scout had replied, but he continued to stare. And a small hurt, hidden far inside Diskan's overgrown frame of flesh and bone, grew.

What a meeting between father and son! But how could Renfry Fentress have sired—*him?* Scouts, assigned for periods of time to planet duty, were encouraged to contract Service marriages. This grew from the need to breed a type of near mutant species necessary to carry on the exploration of the galaxy. Certain qualities of mind and body were inherited, and those types were encouraged to reproduce their kind. So, Renfry Fentress had taken Lilha Clyas as his wife on

Nyborg, for the duration of his assignment there, a recognized and honored association, with a pension for Lilha and a promising future for any children of their union.

In due time, Renfry Fentress had been reassigned. He then formally severed the marriage by Decree of Departure and raised ship, without knowing whether there would be a child, since his orders were a matter of emergency. Eight months later Diskan had been born, and in spite of the skill of the medics, it had been a hard birth, so hard that his mother had not survived his arrival.

He did not remember the early days in the government crèche, but the personality scanner had reported almost at once that Diskan Fentress was not Service material. Something had gone wrong in all that careful planning. He was like neither his father nor his mother, but a retrocession, too big, too clumsy, too slow of thought and speech to be considered truly one of a space-voyaging generation.

There had been other tests, many of them. He could not recall them separately now, only that they were one long haze of frustration, mental pain, discouragement, and sometimes fear. For some years while he had been a small child, he had been tested again and again. The authorities could not believe that he was as imperfect a specimen as the machines continued to declare.

Then he had refused to be so tried again, running away twice from the crèche school. Finally one of the authorities, after a week of breakage, sullen rages, and violence, had suggested assigning him to the labor pool. He had been thirteen then, larger than most full-grown men. They had been just a little afraid of him. Diskan had a flash of satisfaction when he remembered that. But he had known better than to try to settle problems with his fists. He had no desire to be condemned to personality erasure. He might be stupid, but he was still Diskan Fentress.

So he had gone from one heavy work job to the next,

and the years had passed—five, six? He was not quite sure. Then Renfry Fentress had come back to Nyborg, and everything had changed—for the worse, certainly for the worse!

From the beginning, Diskan had been suspicious of this father out of space. Renfry had shown no disappointment, no outward sign, after that first moment of blank survey at their meeting, that he thought his son a failure. Yet Diskan knew that all this existed behind the other's apparent acceptance.

Renfry's attitude became only another "why," giving Diskan almost the same torture as the first "why" had always held. Why did Renfry Fentress take such trouble to search out a son he had never seen? When Diskan had been born and his mother had died, the Scout had been traced by the Service as was the regulation, so that he might express his wishes concerning the future of his child. And the answer had come back, "Missing, presumed dead," an epitaph for many a First-in Scout.

But Fentress had not died in the black waters of space, where a meteor hit had doomed his ship to drift. Instead, he had been picked up by an alien explorer, outward bound on a quest similar to his own, the hunt for planets to be occupied by a rapidly expanding race.

And among the people of his rescuer, Renfry had found a home, a new wife. When he was again able to establish contact with his own people, he had received the now years-old report of his son's birth. Since his new marriage, happy as it was, could have no offspring, he had hunted that son, eager to bring him to Vaanchard, where Renfry had taken his optional discharge.

Vaanchard was wonder, beauty, the paradise long dreamed of by Renfry's species. Its natives were all grace, charm, intelligence governed by imagination—a world without visible flaw, until Renfry brought his son to shatter the peace of his household, not once but many times over!

Diskan dropped his hands from his ears, suffering the discomfort of sound. He held them up to survey the calloused palms, the roughened fingers. In spite of soothing lotions, the fingertips could still snag fine garments, window hangings, any bit of fabric he touched. They could smash, too, as they had tonight!

There was a smear of blood across the ball of his right thumb. So he had more than memory to remind him of what had happened back there, where the bell-toned notes were rising and falling in a wistful pattern of music that was not human but that sang in the heart, was a part of the body. Light, sound, and, now that he had unplugged his ears, he could hear laughter. It was not aimed at him. They were so kind, so intuitive. They did not use laughter as a weapon; they did not use any weapons. They only overlooked, forgave, made allowances for him—eternally they did that!

If he could only hate them as he had hated Ulken and his like! There was a fuel in hatred to feed a man's strength, but he could not hate Drustans, nor Rixa, nor Eyinada, their mother and now his father's wife. You cannot hate those who are perfect by your standards; you can only hate yourself for being what *you* are.

The movement of his fingers enlarged the bead of blood on his thumb. It trickled sluggishly, and Diskan licked it away.

"Deesskaann?"

The lilting song of his name—Rixa! She would come and find him. There would be no mention of shards of gem blue on the white floor. No one would ever mention again a priceless wonder that had been reduced to splinters in an instant after centuries of treasuring. If they had raged, if they had once said what he knew they thought—that would make it easier. Now Rixa would want him to go back with her. *No!*

Diskan stood up. The carved bench swayed. He watched with a second of detached acceptance—was that about to crash into ruins, too? Then he stepped behind the seat, moving with the exaggerated care that had been a part of him ever since he had come to Vaanchard, knowing at the same time it would be no use, that he would trample, smash, blunder, that wreckage would mark any path he would take through this dream world.

He could not retreat to his own quarters; he had done that too many times in the past few days. They would look for him there first. Nor could he continue to hide out in the garden with Rixa on the hunt. Diskan surveyed the lighted building. Music, the coming and going of forms before all those windows, no hiding place unless—

One darkened room on the lower floor— He made a hurried count to place those two windows. He could not be sure, but they were dark and drew him, as a hurt animal might search out a hollow log for temporary shelter.

The tide of his misery ebbed a little as he bent his mind to the problem of reaching that promised retreat undetected. Clumps of bushes dotted the ground, and he could avoid the one glowing statue. Under the music and voices from the house, he heard the trilling call of a night flying varch. A varch! With a little luck—

"Deesskaann?" Rixa was on the path not far from the bench.

He made for the next bush and crouched behind it. Now he centered a fierce concentration on the varch, visualizing the wide green wings with their tipping of gem dust, which created a filmy aura when it flew, the slender neck, the top-knotted head. Varch—Diskan thought varch, tried to feel varch.

Suddenly that call sounded to his right, beginning as a trill and ending in a squeak of terror. The green body flashed out of the shadow, winged toward the path. Diskan heard a second startled cry—from Rixa. But he was on the move, slipping from one bit of cover to the next, until he stood under the nearest of those dark windows, reaching up for the sill. No mistake

13

now—no clumsy fall. Please, no break— just let him get into the dark and the solitude he must have!

And for once, one of his formless prayers was answered. Diskan spilled through the window to the floor, the sweep of curtains veiling him. He sat there, panting, not with physical effort, but with the strain of steeling himself to master his body. It was several seconds before he parted the curtains to inspect the room.

A single low light let him see that he had taken refuge where indeed they might not look for him—the room that was Renfry's. Here were kept the travel disks from his Scout trips, the trophies from his star wandering, all mounted and displayed. It was a room that Diskan had never before had the courage to enter on his own.

On his hands and knees, he crawled from behind the curtains, to sit crouched in the middle of the open space, far from anything he could brush against or knock over. He laced his heavy arms about his upthrust knees and looked about him.

A man's life was in this room. What kind of showing would *his* life make if the remnants of his passing were set on shelves for viewing? Broken bits and pieces, smudged and torn fabrics—and the slow, stupid words, the wrong actions that would not be tangible but that made smudges and tears inside himself and others. Diskan's hands went up again to his head, not to muffle the sighing music, the hum of voices from beyond walls and door, but to rub back and forth across his forehead, as if to ease the dull ache that had been ever present during his waking hours on Vaanchard. But he did not seem stupid to himself, at least not until he tried to translate into action or words what he thought—as if inside him there was a bad connection so that he could never communicate clearly with his own body, let alone with those about him.

There were things he *could* do! Diskan's mouth for the first time in hours relaxed from the wry twist, even shaped a shadow smile that would have surprised him had he at that moment faced a mirror. Yes, he could do *some* things, and not, he thought, too clumsily either. That varch now—he had thought of the varch, and then he had thought of what it must do—and it had done it just as he wished, and with more speed and skill than his own hands carried out any of his brain's commands.

That had happened before, when he was alone. He had never dared try it before others, since he was rated as strange enough without that additional taint of wrongness. He could communicate with animals—which probably meant he was far closer to them than to his own kind, that he was a slip-back on the climbing path of evolution. But the varch had distracted Rixa for the necessary moments.

Diskan relaxed. The room was still, the sounds of merriment more muffled here than in the garden. And this chamber was less alien in its appointments than any other in the huge palace dwelling. The rich fabrics at the window were native, but their colors were not so muted here. They were warmer. And save for one lacy spiral object on the wide desk-table, there were none of the fragile native ornaments. The rack of travel disks might have been taken out of a spacer—perhaps it had been.

He studied that rack, his lips shaping numbers as he counted the disks, each in its own slot. More than a hundred worlds—keys to more than a hundred worlds —all visited at some time or another by Renfry Fentress. And any one of those, fitted into the autopilot of a spacer could take a man to that world—

Blue tapes first—worlds explored by Fentress, now open for colonization—ten of those, a record of which to be proud. Yellow disks—worlds that would not support human life. Green—inhabited by native races, open for trade, closed to human settlement. Red— Diskan eyed the red. There were three of those at the bottom of the case.

Red meant unknown—worlds on which only one

15

landing had been made, reported, but not yet checked out fully as useful or otherwise. Empty of intelligent life, yes, possible for human life as to climate and atmosphere, but planets that posed some kind of puzzle. What could such puzzles be, Diskan speculated, for a moment pulled from his own concerns to wonder. Any one of a hundred reasons could mark a world red—to await further exploration.

Keys to worlds—suppose one could use one? Diskan's hands dropped again to his knees, but his fingers crooked a little. That thinking, which was clear until he tried to translate it into action, picked at him.

A blue world—another Nyborg or Vaanchard. A green—no, he had no desire to face another alien race, and his landing on such a planet would be marked at once. Yellow, that was death, escape of a sort, but he was too young and still not desperate enough to think seriously of that final door. But those three red—

His tongue crossed his lips. For a long while he had drawn into himself, refused to initiate action that always ended in failure for him. There was a key to be used only by a very reckless man, one who had nothing to lose. Diskan Fentress could be considered as such. He could never be content on Vaanchard. All he asked or wanted was what they would not grant him—solitude and freedom from all they were and he could not be.

But *could* he do it? There was the tape, and outside this house, not too far away, was the port. On that landing space were berthed small, fast spacers. For once his background would be an asset. Who would believe that the stupid off-worlder would contemplate stealing a ship when he had no pilot training, when the control quarters of a small ship would be so cramped for his hulking body? It was a stupid plan, but he was stupid.

Diskan did not get to his feet. Intent even now on making no sound, no move that might betray him, on all fours like the animal he believed he was, he reached the tape rack. His big hand hovered over the three red
16

disks. Which? Not that it mattered. His fingers closed about the middle one, transferred it to a belt pocket—but that left an easily noticeable gap. Diskan made a second shift at the rack; now that gap was at the end of the row, in the shadow. If he had any luck at all, it might not be noticed for some time.

He was rising when he heard it, the click of the door latch. Two steps would carry him to cover. Dared he take them? But again, for once, body and brain worked together. He did not stumble over his own feet, lurch against the table to send the ornament crashing, or make any other mistake; he got safely behind the window curtains before the door opened.

TWO

Notwithstanding the half light, the figure that entered shimmered. Frost stars glinted from a wide collar, from a belt of state. Drustans! Diskan flattened himself still closer to the window frame, felt it bite painfully into his thighs, tried to breathe as shallowly as possible. Rixa was bad enough, but to confront Drustans, her brother, would be a double defeat.

The Vaan youth moved with all the grace of his kind to the desk-table and hesitated there for an instant. Diskan expected him at any moment to wheel, face the window, and draw the skulker out of hiding by the very force of his will. There would be no change in the grave concern of his expression, of course. He would continue to be correct, always able to do the proper thing at the proper time and to do it well.

A small smolder of dull anger still glowed in Diskan, perhaps fed by the fact that in this room he had been able to make a decision, to carry it through without mishap. To surrender now to Drustans would be a special sourness.

But if the Vaan had come for Diskan, nosed him out in some manner—and Diskan was willing to concede that these aliens had powers he did not understand—then Drustans was not making the right moves, for his pause by the table had been only momentary. He went on now to kneel at the tape rack.

Diskan's own hand pressed against the belt pocket.

18

Did—could Drustans have picked, out of the air, the theft? Yes, the Vaan's hand was at the slots of the red tapes! But why—how—?

Drustans plucked out one of the disks—the very one Diskan had moved to fill the empty space. Still on his knees, the Vaan tapped the disk with a forefinger and studied it. Then he tucked it into a belt pocket and, as quickly and silently as he had come, left the room.

Diskan drew a deep breath. So, he had not been after him but had come after the tape. And that could mean trouble because of the switch in disks. Suppose Renfry had sent his alien stepson to get the tape for reference. There were at least three men here tonight who would be interested in information on "red" planets—a Free-Trader captain, Isin Ginzar; an attaché from the Zacathan embassy, Zlismak; and another retired Scout, Bazilee Alpern.

And once the mistake was discovered, Renfry would come here—which meant either Diskan must move at once, tonight, or he faced just another ignominious failure, with more shame and humiliation. He could replace the disk in another slot, let them believe a mistake had been made in filing, which was easy enough—but he could not make himself cross those few feet and put back his key, relinquish his plan. He had accomplished this all himself, thought it out, done it. And he was going to follow through—he had to!

There was nothing he wanted to take with him from this house but that which was already in his belt. It was night. Once out of the garden, he could easily get to the space port. He knew the geography of this small strip of territory well enough. And, Diskan realized, if he did not attempt escape now, he never would; he could not nerve himself to another try.

He swung through the window. The garden was a triangle, its narrowest point extending out from the house, and that point gave access to a side street. He looked down at himself. There was a smudge across the breast of his tunic. He was never able to wear clothing for more than a few moments without collecting stains or tears. Luckily, he was dressed very plainly for a feast day, no frost-star collar, none of the splendor Drustans and the other Vaans considered fitting. He might be taken for a port laborer, wandering lost, if he were sighted.

With caution, Diskan worked his way to the spear point of the triangle. The house was very much alight, but it was close to midnight, and they would be serving supper in the banquet hall. Rixa must have long since given up the search for him in the garden. He must use well what time he had.

Somehow he scrambled over the lacework of the wall, meant more as a frame for the garden than any barrier. One sleeve tore loose from the shoulder, and now he had a smarting scratch, oozing blood, above his elbow. His dress boots made no sound on the pavement. Their soft soles were thin enough to let him feel the stone. But that did not matter—he had gone barefoot so long that his feet were tougher perhaps than the fabric of the boots themselves.

This way—to the corner, then to the first side turning—and that led straight to the port. He would enter quite far from the small ships he wanted, but once he was actually at the field, he could manage. This sudden small self-confidence was heady. Just as in the old tales, you obtained a talisman of sorts and then you were invincible. He had his talisman in the belt pocket, beneath his hand, and now there bubbled inside of him the belief that the rest would follow, that he would find the ship and escape—

Such a spacer would be on two controls, one for manual and one for travel tape. Diskan scowled as he tried to remember small details. All ships took off by pattern, and he dared not ask the Control for a particular one. So, he would have to risk the other way— feed in his tape, set on auto-control, go into freeze himself—and just hope. And the steps for that—? Well, Renfry, striving hard to find a common interest between them back on Nyborg while they had been waiting for exit papers, had talked about himself and
20

his work when he discovered Diskan uncommunicative. And Diskan had listened, well enough now, he hoped, to get him off Vaanchard.

The field was lighted in one section. A liner must have just set down within the hour, as there was activity about one sky-pointing ship. Diskan watched closely and then moved forward, walking with a sureness of purpose. He paused by a pile of shipping cartons and hoisted one to his shoulder, then set out briskly on a course that angled toward his goal. To the casual glance, he hoped, he would be a laborer—one of those selected for the handling of cargo for which machines could not be trusted.

He dared not stumble—he must keep his mind on those slim small ships in their cradles ahead. He must think of his arms, of his feet, of his unruly body, and of what he was going to do when he got inside a space lock. He would mount to the control cabin, strap in, feed the tape disk to the directive, then set the freeze needle, take the perlim tablets—

Diskan was under the shadow of a trader before he thought it safe to dump his burden and quicken his pace to a trot. The first two of the smaller ships were still too large for his purpose, but the third, a racer made more for use within this solar system, between Vaanchard and her two inhabitable neighbors, was better—though he did not know if it could be used to voyage in deep space.

However, such a ship could be set for maximum take-off, to wrench him out of the influence of the control tower. And speed was an important factor. For such a ship there would be a watch robot.

Theft was not a native vice on Vaanchard, but all ports had a floating population of which a certain portion was untrustworthy. No racer was ever left without a watch robot. But Diskan had some useful information from Nyborg, learned by watching his companions at the labor depot. Robots were the enemies of the strong-back boys. When rations were scanty or poor, the human laborers had learned ways to cir-

21

cumvent the mechanical watchdogs at warehouses—though it was a tricky business.

Diskan glanced at his big, calloused hands. He had never tried to dis-con a watcher before. That was a task he had believed he was too clumsy to handle, but tonight he was going to have to do it!

He studied the ship in the launching cradle carefully. The port was closed, the ladder up, and the watcher would control both of those. But a watcher was not only there to check invasion; it was also attuned to any change in the ship. Diskan swung down into the cradle, put where the port inspectors had their scanplate. He forced himself to move slowly. There must be no mistake in the false set of the dial he wanted. Sweat beaded his cheeks and chin when he achieved that bit of manipulation.

Up out of the pit—to wait. A grating noise from above marked the opening port. The ladder fed out smoothly. This was it! Diskan tensed. The watch robot, once out of the ship, would sense him instantly, come for him. A watcher could not kill or even do bodily harm; it only captured and held its prisoner to be dealt with by human authority.

And Diskan must allow himself to be so captured to serve his purpose. There was a clatter; the robot swung down the ladder and turned quickly to rush him. A thief would have run, tried to dodge. Diskan stood very still. The first rush of the machine slackened. It might have been disconcerted by his waiting for it, wondering if he had some legitimate reason to be there. Now if he had known the code word of its conditioning, he would have had nothing in the world to fear, but he did not have that knowledge.

A capture net whirled out, flicked about him, drew Diskan toward the machine, and he went without struggling. The net, meant to handle a fighter, was loose about him. He was almost up to his captor when he sprang—not away from but toward the robot. And for the first time that Diskan could remember, his heavy bulk of body served him well. He crashed against

22

the machine, and the force of that meeting rocked the robot off balance. It went down, dragging Diskan with it, but his arm was behind its body, and before they had rolled over, he had thrust one forefinger into the sensitive direction cell.

Pain such as he had never known, running from his finger up his arm to the shoulder—the whole world was a haze of that pain. But somehow Diskan jerked away, held so much to his purpose that he had dragged himself part way up the ladder before his consciousness really functioned clearly again. Those who had told him of this trick had always used a tool to break the cell. To do it by finger was lunacy on a level they would not have believed possible. Diskan, racked with pain, stumbled through the hatch.

Sweating and gasping, he got to his feet, slammed his good hand down on the close button, and then swayed on—up one more level. The wall lights glowed as he went, obeying the command triggered by his body heat. He had a blurred glimpse of the cradle of the pilot's seat and half fell into it.

Somehow he managed to lean forward, to fumble the disk out of his pocket and into the auto-pilot, to thumb down the controls. The spacer came to life and took over. Around Diskan arose the cradle of the seat. His injured hand was engulfed in a pad that appeared out of nowhere. He felt the stab of a needle as the tremble of the atomics began to vibrate the walls.

Diskan was already half into freeze and did not hear, save as a blur of meaningless words, the demand broadcast as those in Control suddenly realized an unauthorized take-off was in progress. He was under treatment for an injured pilot as the racer made its dart, at maximum, up from Vaanchard on the guide of the red tape.

To a man in freeze, time did not exist. Measure of it began again for Diskan with a sharp, demanding clang, a noise biting at his very flesh and bones. He fought the pressure of that noise, the feeling of the necessity for responding to it. Opening his eyes wearily, he found himself facing a board of levers, switches, flashing lights. Two of those lights were an ominous red. Diskan knew nothing of piloting, but the smooth beat of the Scout ship that had taken him to Vaanchard in his father's company was lacking. There was instead a pulsation, an ebb and flow of power on a broken beat.

Another light turned red.

"Condition critical!"

Diskan's head jerked against the padded surface of the cradle. The words were mechanical and came out of the walls around him.

"Damage to the fifth part. Going on emergency for landing! Repeat: going on emergency for landing!"

Substance spun out of the wall to his left. In the air it seemed a white mist. Settling on and about his body, it thickened, became a coating of cushioning stuff, weaving him into a cocoon of protective covering. The trembling beat in the walls was even more uneven. Diskan knew that an emergency landing might well end in a crash that would erase ship and passenger on the instant of impact.

His helplessness was the worst. Simply to lie there in the covering spun by the ship to protect human life and wait for extinction was a torture. He struggled against the bonds of his padding—to no purpose. Then he yelled his need for freedom to the walls pressing in on him as his screams echoed from them.

Mercifully, black closed about Diskan then, and there was an end to waiting. He was not conscious of the fact the ship had entered planetary atmosphere, that the journey tape guided a crippled ship down to the surface of the unknown world.

The spinning ball of the planet lost the anonymity imposed by distance. Shadows of continents, spread of seas now showed on its surface, appeared waveringly on the visa-plate above Diskan's head. A dark world, a world with a certain forbidding aspect, not welcoming with lush green like Vaanchard or with brown-green like Nyborg—this was a gray-green, a slate or steel-hued world.

24

Orbiting, the spacer passed from night to day, to night, in a weird procession of telescoping time. There was a sun, more pallid here, and five moons shedding a wan reflected light on saw-toothed heights, which formed spiny backs of firm land above morasses of swamp and fen, where the shallow seas and land eternally thieved, one from the other.

There were eyes that witnessed the passage of the ship drawing closer to the surface of the world. And there was intelligence—of a sort—behind those eyes, assessing, wondering. Movement began over a relatively wide space—an ingathering such as was not natural, perhaps an abortive ingathering, or perhaps, *this* time— Eyes watched as the spacer, poised uneasily on its tail of flames, began the ride down via deter rockets to a small safety of rock and earth.

The descent was not clean. One tube blew. Instead of a three-fin landing, the spacer crashed, rolled. Vegetation flamed into a holocaust during that crazy spin. Death of plant or animal came in an instant. Then the broken hulk was still, lying on mud that bubbled and shifted around it, allowing it to settle into its glutinous substance.

For the second time, Diskan roused. The dying ship, in a last spasmodic effort, strove for the safety of the life it had guarded to the best of the ability its designers had devised. The cocoon of which he was the core was propelled from the pilot's seat, struck against a hatch that lifted part way and then stuck. The stench of the mud and the burned vegetation brought him to, coughing weakly.

Wisps of torn white stuff blew around his head and shoulders. The fear of being bound and helpless, which had carried over from those seconds before his last blackout, set Diskan to a convulsive effort, which scraped him through the half-open hatch, meant for the emergency escape.

He went head first into the mud, but his shoulder and side jarred brutally against stone, the pain bringing him around. Somehow he scrambled over stuff

25

that slid and sucked at him until there was solid support under his flailing arms, and he drew himself up on an island in the midst of that instability.

Clawing the remains of the cocoon padding from his head, Diskan stared about wildly. The spacer was three quarters under the sucking mud, a flood of which was now tonguing in the hatch through which he had come. Diskan tried to gain some idea of his present surroundings.

The wind was cold, though the smoldering swamp vegetation still gave off a measure of heat. But the fire ignited by the ship was already dying. Not too far away Diskan saw white patches, which he thought might be snow, on a rising spine of rocks. He had known winter on Nyborg and winds as chill as the one now lapping about his body. But on Nyborg there had been clothing, shelter, food—

Diskan gathered up the torn stuff of the cocoon and drew it about his shoulders, shawl fashion. It made an awkward-to-handle covering, but it was a protection. The ship! There should be a survival kit in that— means of making fire, iron rations, weapons—! Diskan slewed around on his rock perch.

There was no hope of returning to the ship. The flood of mud had poured relentlessly into the open hatch; to try to return was to be trapped. Suddenly he wanted solid land, a lot of it, around and under him. And the best place for finding such a perch was the snow-streaked rocky spine.

It must have been late afternoon when the ship crashed, for though there had been no sunlight, there had been the gray of a cloud-cast day to light the scene. But by the time Diskan, exhausted, smeared with icy slime and almost hopeless, reached his goal, it was well into twilight, and he dared not try to move farther, lest a misstep plunge him into the bog into which the ship had now totally disappeared.

He crawled along the broken rock of the ridge, at last wedging himself into a crevice, where he pulled the cocoon fabric about him. The first moon was up, a round green-blue coin against the sky, and its following sister was above the horizon. But neither gave light enough for further travel over unknown territory.

There were reddish coals on the other side of the mud pool, marking the blaze. Diskan longed for a few of those precious sparks now. But there was no fuel to feed them here and no way of crossing to the burned-over land. He squirmed as far as he could into his shelter, misery eating into him.

So—one part of his mind jeered—you thought luck would change when you used your key, that you could make a better future. Well, here is that future, and in what way is it better than the past?

Diskan coughed, shivered, and chewed on that bitter thought. He had his freedom, probably freedom to die one way or another—by freezing tonight, by slipping into the mud tomorrow, by a thousand and one traps on an unknown planet. But another thought warred against the jeering voice—he *had* survived so far. And every moment he continued to live was a small victory over fate—fate or *something* that had crippled him from his birth. He had this freedom—yes —and his life, and those were two things to hold fast to this night as if they could give him warmth, shelter, and nourishment.

THREE

Diskan feared the insidious chill as the night wore on.
He crawled at intervals from the crevice to stamp his
numbed feet and beat his arms across his chest. To
sleep in this creeping cold was perhaps not to wake
again. And each time he so emerged from his poor
shelter, he strove to view by the light of those hurry-
ing moons just what lay about him.

The rocky point rose in a series of outcrops back and
up in a miniature mountain chain. As far as he could
tell, the rest was bog. Twice he heard a howling from
the path the rolling ship had blasted, and once a
snarling, growling tumult, as if two fairly well-matched
opponents struggled. Perhaps the flamed land held
food that attracted scavengers. Food— Diskan's middle
reacted to the thought. He had often known the bite of
hunger in the past, his big frame requiring more substance than had been allowed on several work proj-
ects, but he could not remember ever feeling this
empty!

Food, water, shelter, covering against the wind and
the cold—and all must be found in a world where even
one mouthful of an alien plant or animal could mean
sudden death for an off-worlder. The rations that might
have sustained him, the immunity shots meant to
carry the shipwrecked through such a disaster—all
were gone.

Howling again—and closer. Diskan stared out across

28

the mud pool to that shore where the embers smoldered. There were shadows there, too many of them, and they could hide anything. How long did night last on this world? Time had no meaning when one could not measure it by any known rule.

It began to snow—first in a few flakes that filtered into his crevice to melt on his skin, then more thickly, until Diskan could not see much but a curtain of white. But with the coming of the snow, the wind died. He watched the storm dully. If this drifted, it would cover the bog and make a treacherous coat to hide the mud.

A sharp cry jerked Diskan out of a half stupor. That—that had come from the outcrops behind his refuge! He listened. The swish of the falling snow seemed deafening, as deafening as his fingers had been in his ears back on Vaanchard. Moments passed. The cry was not repeated. But Diskan knew that he had not been mistaken—he had heard a living thing give voice out there. A hunter—or the hunted? Had that been the death cry of some prey?

Panic was colder in him than the chill born of the rock walls about his shivering body. Every nerve cried, "Run!" And yet his mind fought down that fear. Here he had to face only the narrow opening to the white world; he could defend that opening with his two hands if necessary, whereas in the open he might speedily be pulled down.

Time can dull even the sharpest fear, Diskan discovered. There was no second cry. And, though he listened, there were no more sounds out of the night. Finally, before he realized it, there was a slow end to night itself.

Diskan knew it first when he was aware he could see farther. The snow was spread in a wide cover, broken by patches of dark which must mark the liquid surface of the mud. That rocky far shore lost some of its shadows and was growing clearer by the moment. Though no sun showed, day was coming.

He pulled at the tattered stuff of the cocoon. It was

as white, save for a mud stain here and there, as the snow. And he thought he could knot it into a kind of cloak. His fingers were cold and twice as clumsy as usual, but he persisted until he had a crude rectangle he could pull about his shoulders, anchoring the ends under his belt. The mud through which he had wallowed on his escape from the ship had dried on skin and clothing into a harsh blue shell, which cracked and scaled as he moved but which might give him additional protection against the cold.

Most of all he needed food. Recklessly, he had scooped snow from about the crevice and sucked it so that its moisture relieved his thirst. But, as he wavered out of his crack of shelter and down to the edge of the mud pool in a very faint hope of seeing some part of the ship, he faced only a blue surface rimmed with brittle ice-coated stalks of vegetation on one side and a blackened smear on the other.

It was a small thing to catch the eye, a wisp of yellow-white from the black scar. Smoke! Diskan took a quick step forward and then paused. There might be a still-burning coal over there, but traps lay in between.

"Steady—" he told himself, and the spoken words somehow were as comforting as if they had come from lips other than his own chapped ones. "Slow—steady—"

Mud cracked and fell from his shoulders as he turned his head, tried to assess what lay to the right and how far toward the burned ground his present solid footing extended. Stiffly, forcing himself to study each step before he advanced, Diskan climbed around the rocks. The cold of the stone was searing to his hands until he halted, worried loose some strips of the cocoon material, and tied them about his palms. Meant to insulate, it served for protection, though it made his hands more bulky and threatened his holds.

He pulled to the top of one of the rocky pillars and had his first less limited view of his present surroundings. The spine became part of a larger ridge, perhaps the main body of land. Diskan could see the blackened scar of the ship's crash ahead of him. There were spots of the ominous blue mud and tangles of frozen vegetation, but there were also scattered rocks, which provided stepping stones.

"Slow—" Diskan warned himself. "To the right— that block there—that mat of brush—it ought to hold. Then that other rock— Easy now! Hand hold here—put the foot there—"

He could not have told why it was easier to move when he gave himself such orders, as if his body were apart from his mind, but it was. So he kept on talking, outlining each footstep before he took it.

The patches of white snow, he learned, marked more solid footing, but caution made him test each. And once a stone, hurled ahead, proved that caution wise, for the rock cracked through the surface and a blue earth mouth sucked it down.

He had set foot on the black crisp of the burn, felt and smelled the powdery black ashes his weight disturbed, when a cry startled him, brought his attention to the sky. A winged thing swooped and fluttered, the morning light making its coloring a vivid streak, for it was rawly red, with a long neck that turned and twisted in a serpentine fashion, a head with a sharply peaked comb or topknot. And it was big. Diskan estimated that wing spread to equal his own height.

With a second screech, it planed down—but not at him. It headed on into the heart of the burn smear. Then there came another cry, and a second red flier appeared, to settle at the same spot. Diskan hesitated. The smoke lay in that direction, but he did not like the look of those birds, if birds they were. And several of them together could offer trouble.

More squawking ahead. There was a small ridge between Diskan and where they had landed. Now a squall—the same as he had heard earlier in the night—sounds of what could only be a fight. Diskan went on, and from the top of the ridge he looked down into a battlefield from which the morning wind brought a stench that made him gag.

Things lay there where the flames had struck them down. The bodies had been so crisped that he could not tell more than that they were the bodies of large creatures. On the side of the biggest, one of the red fliers had taken a stand, its long neck writhing as it strove to strike with a sword-sharp beak at a smaller four-footed creature that snarled, squalled, showed teeth, and refused to be driven from its feasting. These were four, five—eight at least of its kind—and they moved with a rapidity that seemed to baffle the birds.

Then one of the defenders grew too bold or too reckless. That rapier beak stabbed and stabbed again. The creature fell back in a limp curl, between the bones where it had been tearing at charred flesh. The victory appeared to hearten the red flier. Its neck curved, and it opened its beak to voice an ear-splitting honk. From the air it was answered. Three, four more of its kind flapped into view.

The animals about the carcasses snarled and complained, but they retreated, their rage apparent in every move. With two of the fliers, they had been ready to contend, but a flock they dared not confront.

As they withdrew under the fire of the now attacking fliers, Diskan got a better view of them. But whether they were warm-blooded animals or reptiles, he could not decide. There was certainly a growth of what seemed coarse yellow-green fur down their backbones and the outer sides of their legs, and a bush of it upstanding on their heads, but their projecting snouts, their strongly clawed feet, and their whipping tails were sleekly bare, as if naked of fur but covered with small scales. They were as vicious in appearance as the fliers, and though they were small in size, Diskan had no wish to face a pack of them.

Luckily, their path of sullen retreat was in the opposite direction, up the other side of the cup that held the burned bodies. But though the darting fliers barred them from the ridge on which he stood, Diskan also edged back. He stumbled down through the powdery ash to the hollow from which the smoke still ascended. A handful of what seemed to be stones lay there, and two of them showed a red tinge. Diskan stooped and blew gently. The red deepened—a mineral that the fire had ignited and that continued to hold the heat? He sat back on his heels. Here was the means of fire—warmth—not only to be used here and now, but to be taken with him to a less populated section of the country, if he could find the means to transport one such coal. His resources in that direction were limited.

Under a coat of cracking mud, he wore the tight breeches and ornamented tunic of Vaan festival dress. That did not even permit a ceremonial hunting knife at the belt, as was the fashion on Nyborg. All he had was two belt pockets, one of them empty since he had used the tape.

Pocket! Diskan pulled open the pocket covering. Then he plucked at the raveling patches that served him as gloves, bringing loose a fluff of broken threads. Insulation—of one kind—and there was that of another, too. He went to the edge of the mud pool, worked his threads into the evil-smelling substance of that quaking earth, and, with care, smeared the mixture into the interior of the belt pocket, making sure all of its surface was thickly covered.

Moments later he was ready to go, his hand cupped over the now bulging pocket where that glowing bit of mineral was safe. He had fire, the first weapon of his species, now at his command. And he wanted to get away, as sounds from over the ridge suggested that the ground pack of scavengers had been reinforced and was once more giving battle.

Diskan made his way back to the rock spine. Food—he might have been lucky enough to knock over one of the scale-fur things or a flier—but he was not too sure. And to arouse the rage of either species, presenting himself as a possible meal, would have been folly. But judging by the numbers he had seen, he realized this was not an empty land. He could find other prey.

He passed the crevice of his night camp and began to climb to the promise of wider land beyond. As he crested a slope, he caught a strong scent—not the stench of the scavengers' feast, but certainly not that of vegetation either. It was not disagreeable, and it attracted him enough to want to learn its source.

Diskan's kind had long since lost their dependence on the sense of smell—if they had ever possessed it to the extent of the other mammals that had shared their first home world. What might have been a quickly identified beacon to one of those was an illusive trace for his questing nostrils. But he continued to sniff as he went.

He found the source at a narrow cut between two leaning rocks. On the gray surface of both those pillars was a silvery smear, which glistened in the now strong sunlight. Diskan thought a liquid had been sprayed there, to trickle for an inch or so in fast freezing drops. But between the rocks lay something to capture his attention at once.

The creature was dead, its throat ripped wide, the frozen blood a clot of red crystals. Unlike the scavengers, it was entirely furred, the fur as gray as the rocks about it, so that it was the wound he had first seen. That it was a hunter was manifest by the fangs in its gaping mouth, the claws on its feet. The head was long and narrow, with ears pointed and extending backward. It was short of leg but long of body, well adapted to the rocky country in which it had died. And it was meat!

Diskan jerked the body loose from the ground, finding it lighter than he had thought it would be. He had his meal, thanks to the unknown hunter who apparently had not lingered to consume the kill. With a strip of the cocoon material, he tied two of the limp legs to his belt and went on in search of a camping spot.

It was not too long before he found that. A stiff pull up through a small gorge brought him to an ice-encased stream. And along the bed of that grew the brittle winter-killed growth of more than one small bush and struggling tree.

The withered leaves that clung to a few branches were silvery in color. Diskan wondered as he broke up wood for his fire if that were the normal shade of vegetation on this planet. He coaxed flame from the smoldering mineral and then examined the body of the animal. He had no knife, no way of cutting or cleaning it, of even skinning the creature. There was no resource but to toss the whole thing into the blaze and let the fire work for him.

It was a grim and nasty business, but hunger drove him. And he licked his fingers afterwards, the pain in him stilled for a while—though he wondered if his system could assimilate the alien flesh or if illness and death would come from that eating. From the fire he raked the blackened skull and studied it. The strong, slightly curved teeth caught his attention, and with a rock he smashed the charred bone, breaking out the largest teeth. Two were the length of his little finger, all were sharp, and he thought that they might have future possibilities. Diskan opened the second pocket on his belt and brought out its contents.

A flash writer—he smiled wryly—just what he needed now. His name check plate—for a moment he fingered that, half inclined to toss it away. The code on this thin strip of metal would have brought him food, clothing, lodging, and transportation anywhere on Vaanchard; here it was useless. But he would not discard anything until he was sure. A ring—Diskan turned that around. Its deep purple gem did not flash fire in the sun; it was somber and dark, Diskan's own choice of adornment, though he had hardly looked at it when he had taken it from the box back on Vaanchard. Custom dictated that he wear it. He had squeezed it onto his little finger, the only one the loop would fit, and then dragged it off again, too aware of how incongruous it had looked on *his* hand. It was as useless here as all the rest.

Now he could add to his treasure six teeth, blackened by burning, which might or might not be more serviceable in his present plight than all the other things. He put them back in his pocket, the teeth on top.

His clothing, under the coating of stains and mud, appeared to be standing up well to the rough travel of the morning. Diskan inspected his calf-high boots carefully. There were scuff marks, a scoring or two, but the soles were surprisingly intact. And his cocoon cloak, while a thing of dangling tatters, was still protection.

He was alive; he had food and fire, and he was free. Diskan leaned his back against a piece of water-worn rock and looked at the drift, which suggested that this ice-bound stream had a turbulent past. The riverlet's valley appeared an easier path into the interior of the higher land, and there was plenty of firewood here. He had put aside a haunch of the late meal to provide food for later. And the sun, while not really warm, seemed to concentrate in this cut so that a few of the snow patches were melting.

Save for the dead animal, Diskan had seen no sign of life in this part of the country. Perhaps the feast by the burn scar had drawn most of the hunters. So much on the hopeful side.

On the other hand, this climate was hard, since he was unequipped for it. And this could be only the beginning of a far more severe season, with a long period of steadily worsening weather to be faced. He had no weapons, no knowledge of how long his lump of mineral would continue to smolder or of how much native fauna there was to protest his invasion of hunting territory they considered their own.

Dwelling on the worst would get him nowhere, and the more one permitted one's imagination to summon up difficulties, the darker all shadows became. Diskan began to search through the driftwood about him. It was all bleached, but one piece was enough different in color to attract his attention. He knelt and worked it loose from the frozen soil.

He held a barkless length of what might have been a branch. Thick as his wrist, it had a smooth surface that was not gray-white but a dull green, with the grain marking showing up in a darker emerald. One end was a thickened, knoblike projection, from which stubs of other small growths jutted. The other end was splintered into a sharp point.

Diskan swung it experimentally. Somehow it balanced well in his hand. The knob head could be a club, the splintered end a short, thrusting spear. With a little work, say some way to fasten the teeth to those stubs and a little honing and sharpening of the spear end, he would have a weapon—outlandish and very far removed from a blaster, a stunner, or any of the arms known to stellar civilization, but still a weapon.

Knotting the seared meat to his belt, the bulb-spear in his swathed hand, Diskan strode away from his dead fire. He walked firmly, his head up, his eyes searching the country around him. There was no fumbling in his hold of that weapon, no shambling uncertainty about his pace.

FOUR

Though there were no clouds to screen off the sun's rays, shadows laced the cleft through which the stream issued, and Diskan saw that the walls of that cut rose slowly on either hand. It grew more chill between those barriers, and the frozen growth was scarcer. He had a choice, to halt here for the night where there was still fuel for a fire, or to go on into the unknown on chance. Finally, he decided in favor of the halt.

He had his fire going and was gleaning more fuel for its night feeding when he straightened, his hand going to the club he had thrust through his belt. The sensation of being watched was so sharp that he was disconcerted when he swung about to perceive nothing but the rocks, the frosty earth, and the broken brush. As far as he could tell, there was no hole in the surface of either cleft wall large enough to hide a sizable enemy in ambush.

Yet he was sure that there was something—or someone— lurking there, watching. Diskan pulled his weapon from his belt, making a show of using it to pry a length of drift from the iron-hard hold of the frozen soil. He hoped his sudden about-face had not betrayed his suspicions. It might be a small advantage for him if the hidden one believed he was still unconscious of its presence. But Diskan gathered his wood now with his left hand and kept the club ready in the right.

Twice more he tramped back to the side of the fire

to dump loads. He was trying to locate the source of that spying. No hole in the cliff faces, no growth large enough to mask anything of a size to be feared. Or was that true? There were reptiles, insectile things, small, but still deadly, to be met on other worlds. The same might well be true here. Only Diskan could not associate his feeling of being under observation with the idea of a reptile or an insect. He chose a water-worn rock and set his back against it. Keep it up—this act of unconcern—and do not, he told himself fiercely, do not use what you know to judge what may be met here!

He rubbed his thumb across the knot end of the spear-club. A piece of wood. What kind of defense could it offer against any attacker? Diskan picked at the projecting stubs—three of them shooting at angles. He had had a hazy idea of connecting the teeth to those stubs. But how could they be fitted so? Always he had made a botch of any hand work that required exact fingering.

"Take it slow—" he said, his words a muttered whisper. "Just take it slow—" He blinked into the fire, thinking.

Always—always there had been a pushing at him from without. The impatience of all those quick ones through whose world he had shambled, stumbled, blundered, had beat at him. He had never traveled at his own pace—not that he could remember—except those times when they had left him alone to do some dirty job. And even then there had been surprise supervision from those who made manifest their belief that his efforts would always fall far short of their demands.

Diskan fed the fire as he deliberated over the events of the immediate past. And he grinned with a new confidence at the flames. Why—he must be an outlaw now! He had stolen that ship—and he had no notion how many laws, rules, or regulations he had broken since he had plucked that tape from the storage rack. On the other hand, he had escaped the ship, survived a freezing night, found a road to higher land, had fire, a weapon—though there was that watcher out there. A seesaw balance that the slightest mistake would swing against him—permanently—

Being an outlaw did not bother him. In a way, he had been one since his birth—an outlaw or an outsider. He felt no guilt over the ship. If he had the past hours to live over again, he would do just the same. Past hours! for the first time Diskan was startled to recall that he had no idea how long a voyage the tape had covered. He could have lain in freeze for months. But for him the escape from Vaanchard was only a day or so behind. No use bothering with time—all that counted now was day and night here.

Night was coming. Was that what held the watcher quiescent all this time? Was it a hunter that struck at night? Diskan measured his pile of wood. He had had little sleep the night before, and he was not sure he could keep awake very long now. And if the fire died, the chill might be as dangerous as that watcher. Already the sun had gone from the stream valley, and shadows made dark patches that advanced stealthily toward his oasis of flame and warmth.

Movement! Diskan held the club with a steady hand. Surely he had seen a shadow flit from one rock to another. Animal? If so, could he—

For the first time, he thought of how he had handled the varch. Might he deal with an intruder so? But he had known something of their habits. And he had had failures on Nyborg, trying to handle feral beasts unfamiliar with human-kind.

But—Diskan could not build a mind picture of a shadow. He lacked a goal for his reaching thought. There were the fur-scale creatures, the red fliers, the dead thing that had furnished him with food. He concentrated on a mental image of each in turn and reached—to meet nothing. A shadow was no proper target.

Beyond the limit of Diskan's sense, there was a stir—a heightening of concentration. The shadow quivered, nerve alerting muscle. A sense for which the man had no name went into action. The shadow waited, first eagerly, then impatiently, and then with a dying hope that became resignation. A head moved; jaws opened and closed on something inert. So, the other way—the slower way of contact. A slim body flowed about the rock, dragging a burden with it.

Diskan sat very still. The shadow had taken on substance. A dark blot separated from a rock, advanced toward him with a curious bumping up-and-down movement. Even though the twilight was thickening in the valley, Diskan could make out the outline of the creature's head—and it was misshapen. And then he saw that it was dragging along the limp body of another animal, bumping it over the uneven ground.

On the very edge of the fire gleam, the burden was laid down and the carrier arose in a slender furred pillar. Points of red, bright as any gem on a Vaanchard collar, were steady in a head hardly bigger than the neck that supported it. The creature was large enough so that, holding itself erect on its powerful haunches, its bobbing head could have nosed Diskan's shoulder with him standing. And its whole stance spelled not only power but also complete confidence.

The fur, which was a thick and gleaming coat on its body, was dark, save where the firelight brought small frosty sparkles running along the surface. The front paws, now held against a slightly lighter chest, were equipped with claws of a formidable length.

Diskan did not move; at that moment he could not. Those fangs, showed in a gleaming fringe below the lips, made the threat, and Diskan recognized it. Yet there had been nothing in its approach to suggest that it was about to hurl itself at him. Was it the ruler of this strip of country, so supreme in its ownership of a hunting territory that it did not view him as an enemy to be feared? Curiosity was strong in many creatures. Hunters on Nyborg used fluttering strips of bright cloth tied to a stake to draw in fesil for the kill, since

41

they could not stalk that fleet-footed animal with any hope of getting close enough for a stun blast.

His scent, the fire, his trail could have drawn the attention of the thing now watching him with such cool appraisal. And if he made no threatening gesture, it might withdraw, once its curiosity was satisified. But it settled back on its haunches with a little wriggle, as if it intended to keep its position for a while. Diskan knew very little of animals, save what he had learned through his own untrained observations. But as his first surprise wore off and the newcomer made no move, his own curiosity grew stronger.

It had come on four feet, and he thought that was its normal form of progress. But it also seemed at ease in its present erect pose. And there was something odd about the way it held its forepaws.

The fire needed attention, but dare he move? Any gesture on his part might alarm his visitor—cause it to attack as a startled animal could. Or it might go, and Diskan was suddenly aware that he did not want that either, not until he could learn more about it.

Hoping that once again he could move with sure ease, he put out his hand. But it was the old curse that made him misjudge distance and knock down a pile of branches. Hand grasped club in a spasm of reaction as he waited.

But the visitor did not move. The sinuous head was erect, the red eyes still regarding Diskan. He grabbed for the nearest sticks and thrust them crookedly into the flames. The fire shot up, drawing a flickering veil between him and that silent watcher. When he could see clearly again, the animal had withdrawn a short distance and was again rising on its haunches. But the limp body it had brought still lay where it had been dropped.

Diskan eyed that and his visitor.

"You forgot your supper—" His words sounded too shrill, a little ragged, but to his amazement he was answered.

How could you describe the sound issuing from between those rows of fangs—not quite a hiss, nor a growl either. A soft sound, which, Diskan thought, could be a warning. Again he tensed, waiting for some move of aggression. It was then that a very odd thought flashed into his mind. That animal—it acted as if it expected some special response from him!

What? Had it delivered a formal warning recognized by its own kind—a kind of "get out of my territory or take the consequences" challenge? His ignorance was a danger. How much intelligence watched from behind those red eyes, assessing and reasoning from what the eyes reported? Humankind had long ago learned that intelligence and humanoid shape were not always allied. There were humanoid animals —and nonhumanoid "men." What did he have here?

Diskan's formal schooling had all been at the crèche. His resentment and fear of the impersonal authority exercised there had turned him against learning, and they had written him off as waste material. He had fought mental training as he had fought all the rest of the system in which he did not and could never fit. What he knew had come later, in scraps and bits of observation and pick-up information, when he had realized that he had willfully flung away the good with the bad. Now he had little background to base his guesses upon—and he had no confidnce in such guessing.

Suppose he now confronted intelligence. Would it be an intelligence so far removed from his own type that communication was impossible? How could you say this creature "reasons," is a "man," and that one is what his own species declared an animal?

"I mean you no harm—" The words sounded silly even as he mouthed them. To a creature who might communicate in hisses and growls, they could have no meaning. There was a gesture, universal among *his* kind—would it convey anything to the visitor? Diskan raised his hands, palms out and on a level with his shoulders—the old, old "See, I bear no weapons against you; I come in peace."

There was no answer; the red eyes did not even blink. Diskan dropped his hands. That had been as stupid as his oral appeal. Of course the gesture would mean nothing. Yet he had a strong urge to persist, to try to make contact, for the more he considered the creature's behavior, the more he was sure that it was not the ordinary curiosity of a wild thing—not even that of a hunter that feared nothing within its own country—that held it there. Could he approach it?

Diskan shifted his weight, about to rise. Then he remained still, for his visitor had swung its head around. It no longer faced him. Instead, for a long moment, it gazed over its shoulder, down the now dark ravine. Then it dropped to four feet, and with a litheness almost serpentine, it simply flowed between two large stones, to vanish into the night.

Although Diskan waited, trying to catch any sound above or beyond the crackle of the fire, he heard nothing. Yet he was certain that the creature had been alerted, or summoned, and that it had left with a very definite end in view. When waiting did not bring its return, Diskan moved beyond the fire to the prey it had left behind. Again he picked up one of the long-eared, short-legged animals, its throat torn. But this was not frozen. It must have been killed only a short time ago.

Well, his visitor's loss was his gain. Here was more food—though he wanted to devise a less messy way of cooking it. Some experimentation with the sharp end of the club-spear proved that its point could function as a knife. And with that poor aid, Diskan was able to worry off the skin and clean the beast. He impaled it on a piece of drift and roasted it to make a better meal than the burned meat that had sustained him that morning. He left a portion untouched and on impulse carried that to where he had last seen the creature, laying it on the ground there. The stranger might not care to have its food seared, but he would make the offering.

Diskan kept awake as long as he could, feeding the

44

fire. The heat, reflected against the rock he had chosen as part protection, made him drowsy, and at last his head fell forward, to rest on his knees. But the club-spear lay under his hand, free and ready.

A furred head moved from the shadows into the open. There was no need for its owner to sniff at what lay there. Lip wrinkled up over fangs in distaste; the burned flesh was decidedly not to its taste. Then the head rose a little, and eyes noted the fire, the sleeper on its far side.

So, some contact, the furred one thought. This—this other had accepted food; that much it had responded. It was a matter of waiting. The carrion eaters downstream—it would be a long time before they would again follow this trail! Satisfaction, hot and complete, blanketed other thought for a second. Watch—watch and make sure this one followed the right trail. Perhaps, only perhaps—

Stern admonition against such speculation followed. Remember the other failures. But this one was different. His general shape is the same, to be sure. Shape—what matters shape? This one responded differently.

The silent discussion the furred one had with itself came to an abrupt close. The furred body coiled into a circle with muzzle rested on strong hindleg. Something lighter than sleep, but resting body and mind, claimed the watcher for a space. Diskan's sleep was far deeper as the fire smoldered to gray ash.

He was pulled out of those depths, feeling cold and stiff. The fire was a black dead ring, and it was snowing again. The wet of the melting flakes was on his face as he looked blearily about. Stumbling up, Diskan stamped his feet, their numbness alarming him. He swung around to where he had left the meat offering.

Snow had drifted over it, but he could still see a greasy end of bone protruding. He walked over to pick it up—frozen hard, and there was no sign that it had been touched. He could not have explained why he was disappointed. He should be pleased, Diskan told

45

himself. The visitor had probably not returned, and his food supply was increased by so much.

The snow was growing thicker. Might be well now to get out of the open, keep on down the narrowing end of the ravine where the walls arched toward each other almost like a roof. He made a bundle of unburned wood, bowing his back under it, and club in hand, pushed on.

Around him the white surface was unmarked by any track, though Diskan kept a lookout for any trace of a paw trail. He had been right about the cover offered in the narrows; the drive of the snow failed as he advanced. However, the footing here was not so good. Evidences of raging high water through this gorge were present in tumbled stones and bedded drift that protruded just enough to provide trip traps. Diskan's pace grew slower and slower.

It was dark in here, too. He could look up to a slit of sky, but yesterday's sun was missing, and the heavy clouds turned day into twilight. Once he paused to consider the advantages of retracing his way into the open, where the brush would give him fire and he could hole up for the storm to pass—always supposing that it was not of the variety to last several days. But even though he faced about and took a step or so along that back trail, Diskan discovered it made him increasingly uneasy to retreat, and finally he plodded doggedly on.

An increase of falling snow marked the beginning of an opening from the gorge, and he came out into a space where the water was no longer a stream but a small lake. Ropes of ice threaded down a cliff face to his left, marking a falls. The same gray dead growths grew here, but there was also a small stand of trees that were not leafless. Instead, they presented a brilliant patch of color.

Neither scarlet nor crimson but a shade between the two, which Diskan could not name, the wide leaves rattled against each other as the wind blew. He caught a metallic note; the leaves might be some hard sub-

46

stance. More of them lay in bright patches under the trees. Diskan saw some, detached by the present breeze, fall—as if their weight bore them directly to the ground, not fluttering away at the wind's pleasure.

The red wood was on the opposite side of the lake, but it drew Diskan, as if its color was a warmth. He crept across a bridge of ice-rimmed rocks, seeing below the frozen surface the water swirling to the stream that had guided him. When he came to the first of the trees, he noted that each of those brilliant leaves was coated with a transparent shell of ice, making hard winter gems. And their sharp edges could cut—he drew back from that danger.

As he opened his belt pocket for the coal, Diskan examined the small lump anxiously. To his eyes, it seemed just as it had been when he had first picked it up—its power to ignite in no way diminished. But it could not continue so forever, and could he find another such? He had seen it only as a coal and had not the slightest idea of how to search for its like in the natural state.

Diskan dropped his bundle of wood. He need not have lugged that along; there was plenty here. But again prudence had dictated that he go prepared. Fire first, and then food, then—

Sometime he would have to set on a goal, not wander aimlessly. Find a place for a semipermanent camp, then hunt and— Diskan shook his head. Fire now. Go easy—one thing at a time.

FIVE

Red and silver—as if fire and ice had combined weirdly to raise such walls, for this was a city, and through it moved shapes which were only fluidly flowing shadows, never to be clearly seen. Yet they went with a purpose Diskan could dimly sense, though it was not any purpose of his or his kind. Moreover, the urgency that was motivating the shadows reached out to him, enfolded him, making him uneasy, not knowing the why—only that he was drawn deeper and deeper into the heart of fire and ice, there to witness, or to partake, in some crucial rite.

Sometimes as he followed those shadows, a piece of the city would loom clearly before him for an instant of sharpened sight, and he would glimpse a bit of carving, a doorway, a flight of steps that were real and solid amid the dream. But though he fought to reach such, as they seemed islands of safety in the curious liquid life about him, yet he was always borne swiftly by on a river with a current he could not oppose.

Then sound joined sight, a sound he could not define any more than he could define the nature of the shadows. And that sound was a part of him, striking to his very bones, knitting him into the city and its purpose, until Diskan knew the birth of panic. More wildly he fought to break the pull of the current, to win out of the flow.

Sight, sound, and now scent—a scent about which there was a faint familiarity. There, in one of the patches of clear visibility, was a pillar—or was it a tree, a tree with bright red leaves? Diskan made a mighty effort. If he could throw his arms about its bole, he could free himself from the current.

Did his reaching fingers feel the texture of bark? The sound beat in his ears now like the pulsing of his own heart as the city became a wild swirl of red and silver, silver and red, until the colors made one.

But still his fingers held something— Gasping, Diskan came to himself. He was standing calf deep in the snow, his roughly mittened hands clasping the trunk of one of the trees, while the frozen leaves overhead chimed in the wind. Under the racing moons, the ground was light in its snow blanket. He could see the sharp division between shadow and open.

His fire burned as a single red eye. Yet from it curled a plume of smoke that was not the yellow-white of normal burning. It was visible against the snow bank because of the tiny dancing red motes caught up in it. They sparkled in small flashings of light as they ascended.

Diskan pulled out of the snowdrift and staggered back to the fire. There was a scent to that smoke, cloyingly sweet, and it lapped out a tongue to meet him. Coughing, waving a hand before his face to clear the motes from him, he circled to the other side. There was evidence of what had been fed to the fire, skeleton now, but still to be seen—leaves from the grove.

He picked up a branch and stirred those skeleton leaves into broken ash. The glowing bits gave forth one last burst of spark motes. Diskan gulped frosty air into his lungs. Everyone dreamed, of course, but the fantasy from which he had just awakened was unlike any other dream he had ever had. It had been so real, in spite of its vagueness of detail. Had the leaf smoke been responsible for it?

Warily, he searched through the pile of firewood, putting aside any which might have originated in the nearby trees. Then he coaxed the flames to full life again, sure of danger in such dreaming. He had been quite far away from his fire when he had awakened. What if he had wandered farther yet and succumbed to the numbing cold before he roused?

Yet as he squatted by the fire, Diskan could not erase memories he had carried out of the dream. Unlike those from ordinary dreams, they did not fade but grew sharper as he dwelt upon them. Those momentary clear glimpses he had had of the city, of a carven block set in a wall— The markings on that block, he had seen them only in the dream— A doorway that he *knew* gave upon stairs, he had not sighted—

Diskan shook his head. Beyond those bits, nothing. Yet there was a vast importance to them. He would never forget them, purposeless as they might be.

The day broke clear with the coming of sun instead of another fall of snow. Diskan ate the last of the meat. Though it would have been prudent to save some scraps for the future, once he had begun to gnaw the hard flesh, he finished it.

By the time the sun was well up, he had discovered that the valley about the falls and the lake was a prison. To climb up the ice-coated surface of the cliff by the falls was a feat he dared not attempt. Beyond the wood was another sharp rise, so he was in a cup with only one entrance and exit, the stream gorge he had followed the night before. Yet every time he turned to that, he was stopped as effectively as if he ran into a barrier. What or why that was, he did not know, just that *that* trail was closed to him.

That left only the valley walls to explore. By midday, he settled on what he deemed the best ascent, a place behind the grove. There was more of a slope there than elsewhere. His old dread of his clumsiness was in full force, and he was sweating in spite of the cold as he dragged himself up to a ledge about three times his own height above the valley floor. Remembering the most elementary precaution about not looking down, he scraped along the ledge, hugging the cliff, studying each step ahead before he planted boot on it.

Not too far away, that scanty footing widened under a broken patch of rock, offering the possibilities of a rough ladder. He gained that point and surveyed the way ahead. The roughened surface did not rise straight up but diagonally. Only when he pushed a little away from the cliff surface to look up, Diskan could see a snow hang there. To have that start a slide—

Diskan caught the tip of his tongue between his teeth and tried to breathe more evenly. His imagination had been only too quick to produce a picture of instant catastrophe. And it was in a spirit of defiance against his own body that he reached up for the first hold.

He had never doubted his own strength, only his use of it, but the climb was an ordeal that tried every bit of stubborn endurance he possessed—not by its difficulty, for the hand and foot holds were there and he found them, but by his abiding fear of not using them properly, or making some awkward slip through his own clumsiness.

Now his field of vision was rigidly limited to a few feet, but he was always aware of the overhang of snow that could sweep him in an instant from the path he so painfully traveled. The pads of cocoon material bound about his palms absorbed the perspiration on his hands, but his face was dripping with sweat, his fair hair plastered to his skull. And now and then he had to rub his head against his arm to clear his eyes of the stinging salt moisture.

A study of the way ahead showed that he must edge along an almost horizontal crack that sloped to the right. But it was here that the menace of the snow hang was the greatest. Diskan's arms trembled with effort, and it seemed to him that his body was more and more sluggish. But there was no retreat now.

He grunted and pulled to the right, into the crack. A four-inch surface, surely not wide enough to be deemed a ledge, was under the toes of his boots. And above, at shoulder level, there were hand, or at least finger, holds. With his body pressed tight to the frigid stone, so that his cheek was scrapped by the surface of the rock, he could move, inches at a time.

Inch out, pull over, inch out, pull over—the nightmare journey went on and on. He was shaken out of his terrible absorption in winning those inches, one at a time, when he felt a wider surface under his boot soles. The crack ledge was broadening! With a gasp of relief, he moved faster and then slowed under sharp control. This was no time to take a chance!

The poor bit of hope he had carried with him from the valley floor was swept away in an instant as he rounded a spur of the wall. The ledge widened—to a good-sized shelf— then ended! Nor was there any hope he could see of another way up that last pull to the top of the cliff. Diskan collapsed, his lips trembling a little as he faced defeat.

What was worse, he was sure that he had no retreat either. He could not control the shaking of his hands, a shaking that spread up his arms and into his body, while he tried to control convulsive shudders born of fatigue and tension. He pulled up his legs and drew in upon himself in a ball of fear and despair.

A fine sifting of snow filtered down to powder him. That overhang—would the wind bring it down? Diskan roused from his fog of misery. If he could not go forward, he would *have* to go back, and he had better try that before inaction and cold froze his nerves and muscles and he could not do it at all.

He pulled up to his feet, turned to face left, and was feeling for the first step back when he saw a dark blot flattened against the cliff as he was. Fur fluffed under the exploring fingers of the wind, but clawed feet clung tightly, and those eyes—not reddened now by fire gleam but in their way still gem-bright—were on him. The creature of the wild was coming along the ledge path.

Diskan could not raise his club now, and even as he watched, the dark blot moved and gained a good length
52

in his direction. It paused again, still eying him. That stare robbed Diskan of what small confidence he had managed to dredge up. He pushed back onto the wide portion of the ledge and shouted, in what was part defiance but more surrender to unavoidable fate.

He fell, scrabbling wildly for a hold to keep from going over the edge. Then the animal landed beside him, half on him, and he heard the roar of the snow giving way. Diskan always wondered how that rush from the heights missed sweeping them along, but the center of its force was farther to the left, over the section where he had traveled one inch at a time. Snow buried him, but he was still on the ledge when the fury of the slip was past, its final crash in the valley loud in his ears.

He felt hot breath on his cheek and smelled a scent like that of the smears on the rock where he had found the body of the first kill. Diskan looked up into those eyes only inches away from his own as he lay on his back. Breathing hard, he kept still. That fanged mouth was too close to his throat, and he remembered the wounds that had torn the life out of its prey.

Then that furred head snapped back, and the creature pulled away from him. But Diskan did not move until it had withdrawn to the other end of their small perch. With all the caution he could summon, he sat up, his back against the cliff, his feet out over space.

The animal did not move. It had risen on its haunches, erect as it had sat across the fire. And its attention was divided between the man and the situation in which they found themselves. Diskan shivered. The snow slide had carried away the threatening overhang, but he knew that he could never turn his back on the animal to shuffle along the narrow crack.

When his companion in misfortune made no other move, Diskan relaxed a fraction. He eyed it measuringly. In the firelight and during his first glimpses of it here, it had seemed dark. But now the wind ruffled the long fur on its back and shoulders, and there were

53

frosty streaks revealed, as if, close to the skin, the silky hairs of the pelt were far lighter in shade. The color was a slate gray with a blue cast, a shade or so darker than the rocks behind it, lighter on the belly and the inner sides of the legs. All in all, it was a handsome animal, even if its movements suggested a power approaching viciousness.

"Where do we go from here?" Diskan asked at last, his voice breaking the silence sharply.

The narrow head snapped about. Then it turned again with what seemed calculated deliberation—so that the animal looked at the cliff face that kept them both marooned.

For the second time, it looked to Diskan, then back to the cliff. The man frowned. To read any meaning into those gestures was sheer imagination, but it would appear the animal was striving to force his attention in that direction.

"No road there," Diskan returned. "I've already looked—"

Once more the head swung back, eyes on him, drawing his gaze to them. Diskan broke that contact with a little cry. He did not know what had happened then, only that he feared it and that he wanted no repetition of that strange sensation.

For the first time, the animal uttered a sound, a hiss that held overtones of anger as far as Diskan could guess. Then, with the same deliberation of its head turns, it crossed to the edge of the ledge, turned, lowered its hindquarters, and hung so, wriggling its body, for several seconds. It might have been searching for claw holds it knew were there—then it vanished from sight.

"What—?" Diskan crawled to the place where it had disappeared, fighting a dizzy feeling as he looked over.

The animal was climbing along the rock face, working its way with assured purpose and a better rate of speed than Diskan dared try. Having reached a point some distance from the ledge and below it, it began to climb again. When it was on a level with that outcrop, it hissed at Diskan, and he could no longer deny his belief that it strove to show by example the road out.

"I don't have any claws," Diskan protested. "You're better equipped for this than I am." But there was a way along there— Only, with the animal now gone, he could retrace the other way.

The animal was climbing again. A burst of speed brought it to another ledge, and it reared up there, watching the man. There was something so superior in its attitude that Diskan was stung.

"All right—here goes!" Why he was making this insane effort, he did not know, but to turn tail and edge back under the watchful eyes of the animal—he could not do it! Where the furred one had gone, a man was going to follow.

Part of it was bad. As he pointed out, he had no claws, and his fingers and booted toes were far less effective than the natural equipment of his new companion. Once he slipped and thought that his finish, until his fingers caught another hold. After an eternity of struggle, he crawled up to the second ledge—to find it empty. Only in the snow along its steadily widening surface was the firm print of clawed feet leading to the right. Diskan humbly followed. He might have passed the exit from the valley—another rock crevice—had it not been marked for him. The scent was stronger this time than it had been by the kill, for the glistening streaks on the rock were still wet.

Diskan squeezed into that crack. It was a very tight fit, and his cocoon cloak caught on projections and tore yet more, as he took some painful scraps. Then a last jerk brought him out in the open at what must be the top of the valley wall.

Wind had swept the snow from the more exposed positions, and the animal prints held only in the hollows. The surface of this upland was broken, all spires and points. Diskan could look down into the lowlands, where there was a wide sweep of bog, the blue of mud lakes startlingly visible against the gray and white of the rest of the country.

Food—Diskan thought of his stomach for the first time since beginning the climb. There might have been something worth hunting in the valley. Up here there was nothing at all. To go down now into the bog country would be a wise move. He started to pick a path along the heights.

A flash drew his attention to the left, away from his goal. It was something not natural to this rocky land. He could not have told why he was sure of that. Not fire—what would fire be doing here unless he was not alone in his occupancy of this planet? In spite of his hunger, he turned away from the slope that ended in the bog country, to hunt down the source of that flash.

Pattern—those blinks were coming in a pattern! Diskan broke into a trot as he came to a relatively level space. Pattern meant a signal!

He skidded out onto a small open square and stood looking up at the thing that had drawn him. Sometime —very long ago, he thought, as he noted the weatherworn edges of the stone—someone, or something, had chiseled and cut one of the natural rock pinnacles into a squared column. At a little below its crest, an oval of white opaque substance gave forth, at intervals he could time by counting, flashes of clear light.

Five counts, then a flash, three counts, flash, ten counts, flash, eight—then the whole pattern over again. This was a signal. The why Diskan could not tell—for some long vanished aircraft, for communication between distant points of land? But it was very old, and it was the work of intelligence.

So, it could be that he was not alone, that more than his animal visitor had once moved with purpose along this rocky spine.

Diskan walked around the column. In a patch of snow on the other side was a single clawed footprint, a signature and a signpost. And beyond, as timeworn as the columns, were the traces of a way, cut here and there through the rock, leading along the crest of the heights.

It was stupid to turn away from the bogs with their

promise of food, as stupid as anything he had ever done, Diskan told himself. But his boots had already trod on that pawmark, and he knew that he was going to follow that very ancient road.

SIX

At times in the growing twilight, Diskan could not be sure that he was still following any path at all. But then he would sight a marker, a side of rock smoothed to make the passage easier, a flattened length under foot. And the road was descending, not along the bog side of the ridge but on the left where lay higher ground. He sighted other valleys like that which held the lake, level bottoms covered with banks of snow, a few with groves of the red-leaved trees.

It was into the widest of these valleys that the ancient road curled. And the end of that path was marked by two pillars, squared as the one that had borne the signal light. On their crests were lumps, the meaning long since battered away by time. And beyond lay nothing but unbroken reaches of snow. To the left and right, running along the base of the ridge, was a tangle of vegetation, a promise of shelter.

Diskan saw tracks there, not those of the clawed feet, but smaller and rounded as if what made them walked on a foot close to a hoof. Only he was not to follow that, for out of the still air a voice spoke.

The words were unintelligible, but they were words, and that they were meant to catch his attention, Diskan did not doubt. Almost on reflex, he threw himself into the cover of the brush, hugging the earth, staring out into the dusk. He was sure that the call had come from before him, somewhere out of the valley, and not echoing down from the rocks at his back.

There was silence, twice as deep. Diskan lay, watched, and waited. Half unconsciously, he began to count under his breath, as he had with the light flashes on the heights. He had reached thirty when again that spoken sound rolled across the open. On the third repetition, he was sure of one thing—that each time the sound had been the same, that the strange words had been repeated and the tone was mechanically level, as if some machine rather than any living thing had voiced that warning or greeting or summons.

Which of the three it might be had vast importance. To disregard a warning might be high disaster. To answer a summons could be going into peril. But a greeting was something else. And was that broadcast as old as the beacon above? The words were spoken with a crisp, sharp authority. Diskan could not connect it in his mind with the evidences of age at the signal pillar and along the road.

Here was a screen of brush. He could move behind it along the valley wall. If he had been sighted and that voice directed at him, sooner or later that which spoke would come hunting. Diskan moved, his club-spear to hand, his attention fixed on the open.

The broadcast continued to sound at the same intervals as he worked his way from one piece of cover to the next, and it did not vary. But Diskan's uneasiness was not lulled by that fact. The words might be mechanically produced, but that did not mean that he could be sure he was not under observation.

It began to snow again, and he welcomed that together with the dark. Both made a curtain behind which he could move faster. The wall of the valley was curving, and he believed that the voice sounded closer.

He rounded a spur and looked out into another stretch of open. But here there were no bushes, save for some withered stalks very close to him. And the look of those—Diskan pushed out his club and caught the nearest stalk. At a very slight pressure on his part, it snapped, and he pulled it to him.

Burned! It had the same appearance as the seared vegetation he had seen near the crash of the spacer. He rubbed the charred stick between thumb and fore-finger and eyed that open space narrowly. Level—unusually level—more so than any other site he had seen in this new world. A good place to plant a ship. Was that it? Could this be where a spacer had finned in and then lifted again? Snow covered any rocket scars, but it was just possible his guess was right.

Once more that unintelligible message rang through the still air, though now it sounded somewhat muf-fled, as if the falling snow deadened the broadcast. Diskan stood up, daring now to take the chance.

He plunged forward, across the narrowest end of the open expanse, blundering into more burned brush on the far side. Then he saw through the dim light a half bubble that was a familiar thing from his own past. That was a temporary shelter such as he had seen in the tri-dee tapes. It was windowless and doorless, but somewhere along its surface, an entrance would yield to the heat and pressure of a hand. This was a rescue cache, established as a refuge for the survivors of some ship crash. Perhaps more than one spacer had fallen into a mud bog on this unknown world.

And Diskan could understand the need for that broadcast now, even if he did not know the words. It was a set signal to draw any survivors to the refuge. And surely, since the call still sounded, the cache cabin was not in use.

With numb fingers and his teeth, Diskan ripped the cocoon windings from his hand and set it against the surface of the cache at waist level, slipping it along the bubble as he began circling the shelter. Unlike a more permanent erection, any seal would be attuned to the general body heat and not to a palm pattern of an individual man or men. When he found the lock, it should yield to him. Then, food, clothing, arms—perhaps everything he needed—would be his.

How long had this stood here broadcasting its call? And why had it been left? A ship downed here, sending out an SOS—then arrival of a rescue force, perhaps a Patrol cruiser? unable to find any survivors, but evidence that such had existed, had they set up the cache and blasted off, expecting to return later? He could string those guesses together into a plausible explanation—except for the fact that the broadcast was *not* couched in Basic, as it should be for a Service rescue cache.

Diskan had a poor education, but Basic, as well as native planet speech, was hypo-taught to every child as soon as he began to talk. And there were no space-going people now, human or nonhuman, who did not use Basic as the common tongue, though it might be necessary for some aliens to resort to mechanical means for translation. So, why not Basic for the beacon call of a cache?

His questing hand suddenly slipped into a hollow his eyes could not distinguish in the fabric of the cache. It did not feel large enough, that hollow, but he pressed his bare palm as tightly as he could into the narrow space. He had found the lock—now for the unlocking.

A slow glow spread up the walls. Then, as abruptly as a snap of fingers, a narrow slit opened before him, and Diskan edged through—into light, heat, smells. The wall closed behind him as he stood looking about the refuge.

Food—he wanted that first. Diskan took a step or two away from the now resealed door, and then his legs gave out, and he swayed and fell. The light was dazzling; it hurt his eyes. He levered himself up on his hands, to blink at the array of containers jumbled altogether, as if hastily dumped.

Pulling himself to the nearest, a broad cylinder, Diskan forced up the snap lid. More containers, rammed in carelessly. Among them he recognized one, pried it out of the confusion, and triggered the small button on its side.

Minutes later he was gulping a reviving liquid that tasted like a richly flavored stew and that was intended,

Diskan knew, as Sustain food for survivor use. Having finished its contents, he returned to the unpacking of the cylinder. But as he handled each tube, can, and box he pulled from that inner disorder, his surprise grew, and with it an uneasiness.

Some of these supplies he knew, but most of them he did not. Not only that but the unknown items varied among themselves, too. He was sure that the strange identification symbols differed greatly, so that he might now be sorting over rations for a score of races, even of species. Did that mean that the survivors these were intended to succor had been a mixed lot—alien, human, and grades in between? But only a crack liner would carry so widely differing a set of passengers on just one voyage.

And the loss of such a liner would have been news reaching even to Vaanchard. Or—Diskan frowned as he set out that bewildering array of containers—or had such a crash occurred as he voyaged in freeze through space?

But a liner carried a thousand or more passengers. This cache could not contain supplies for that many. Had one lifeboat with a highly mixed crowd set down here? That might be it. Only—why not then broadcast in Basic? It did not fit.

And none of the rations he did know bore the seal of the Patrol—which they surely would have done had this been a Service cache. The way they had been slung into this cylinder, not packed, but crammed— Diskan began to sort them. Surely there was more than one unknown tongue on the Jabels. He pressed the heat-serve button on a second tube and ate its contents slowly, while he studied the display. When he had finished, he restored the unknown rations to the cylinder.

Then, methodically, he began to rummage through the other containers of the cache—to discover that all but three of those were palm-sealed to a personal print code! Then this could not be a Service cache or all contents would be free to anyone managing to make the shelter! This was a cache, right enough, but intended not for any survivor of a space disaster—no, for some special survivors.

Some of the things he had uncovered he could use. There was a parka-coat of Orkanza hide with an inner stuffing of insulating Com moss—a little tight across the shoulders, but he could wriggle into it. Boots of the same Orkanza hide made watertight by sal-fat grease were too small. Regretfully, he had to set those aside. Pushed down under them was a tunic. Diskan spread that out across his knee, and his uneasiness sharpened.

This was a dress tunic, a refinement of Ozackian spider silk—or something quite close to that fabulous, and very expensive, fabric. There was a tracery of embroidery about the high collar and around the breast latches that made a lacy pattern composed of hundreds of minute gems threaded on the silk. Only a Veep would wear a garment such as this. Yet there was a spot on the front, a stain that was greasy to the touch, as if food had been carelessly spattered there.

Diskan folded the tunic and put it with the boots. He found two sleep bags, both too small, but which, put together, would give him a better bed than he had known in many days. But—there were no weapons, no tools, unless both were in the locked boxes. He had food, a new coat, and a big puzzle.

He tried to pry open one of the sealed boxes, using the sharpened point of his improvised spear, only stopping when the wood seemed likely to crack. Primitive as that weapon was, it had to serve him, since the cache could not offer better. Diskan padded the two bed rolls together and then set about moving some of the containers so that anyone entering the shelter would take a tumble to announce his arrival. He stretched out on the bed with a sigh of satisfaction.

In spite of the light still glowing in the walls, he slept—but not to wander in a dream city. Outside the core of warmth, the snow continued to fall, blotting out his own tracks to the cache.

But in the night, others were astir; communication traveled, but not by spoken word. Forces met, moved, parted. Impatience, anger colored the discussion. And then watchers settled into place around the cache and what it held—so important to their purposes.

Diskan stirred, rolled over, blinked at the shaky pyramid of boxes of which he had made his alarm. The light of the walls remained the same—but something was different. He sat up and looked around the bubble with more sharply focused attention. As far as he could remember, it was the same. Surely no one had tried to enter, or that box pile would have fallen.

Quiet enough—that was it, quiet! The broadcast that had drawn him here had ceased to function. He no longer heard that murmur of sound, reduced to a hum by the walls of the shelter. Perhaps his entrance had stopped it.

Why that was making him wary he did not know. But now, trying to remember what had happened up to the point of his falling asleep, Diskan was sure that that murmur *had* continued after he had entered the bubble. So, his entrance had not automatically silenced it.

He had never believed that he possessed too vivid an imagination, but now it seemed to him that the silence of the broadcast could act as a signal by its very absence. Suppose, just suppose, that somewhere else on this world there was a settlement or camp, in automatic communication with the cache—so that when it was entered, the camp was notified. A cache could also be a trap!

Diskan went to the pile of rations and then took up the torn cloak of cocoon stuff, tying it into a bag into which he crammed the supplies. The thought of a trap had settled so in his mind that he thought it a fact. Why it had been set, and for whom, did not matter; getting out of it at once did.

With the parka tight about his shoulders and chest, the bulky bag and his club in his hands, he set his palm to the door. The slit opened, and he came out into day and snow that was knee deep.

No matter what, he was going to leave tracks through this unless another storm covered them. There was a grove of trees before him, not the red-leafed kind, but a mass of a bare-branched, thick-standing species. To get into that grove could mean losing all sense of direction. He must keep in the open and head for the heights from which he had come. In and among those rocks spires would be a good many hiding places.

Having made his decision, Diskan struck out through the puffy snow. It was far harder than it had first seemed, this tramping through drifts. The snow was damp and heavy, clinging to his legs, working into the tops of his boots, caking on the edge of the parka. Twice he fell when footing suddenly sank under him. But he kept going, past the space where he was sure an off-world ship or ships had set down, heading for the rock wall and those eroded pillars marking the ancient road.

He was perhaps two-thirds of the way to that goal when the beacon voice spoke, startling him so much that he lost his balance for a third time and toppled into a drift high enough to engulf him. As he fought his way out, he listened. Were those the same words he had heard the night before or were they different? Diskan discovered that he could not depend upon his memory. They could be different—first announcing his coming and now his going.

But to put on more speed was impossible; he could wade at hardly more than a strolling pace. And twice, when he halted to breathe, he studied the way ahead anxiously. There seemed to be any number of pillar-like formations, all crowned with lumps of snow. Then he knew he was lost.

All right, he did not really need the pillars. At any climbable point, he could find a way back up the slope, and from there he could watch the cache through-out the day. Then, if there were no visitors, at night-fall he could return to shelter in it. Up there, he could watch his own back trail, be sure he was not hunted.

To any Patrol officer, he would be a prisoner, but he was sure that the cache was not Patrol. Perhaps to anyone else, he could pose as a survivor from a life-boat landing. Diskan smiled. He had all day to think up a good story and settle all its details so deeply in mind that he could reel it off with convincing force. He began to climb.

Three times he moved before he found what he deemed the perfect lookout. Though he had no farsee-ing lenses, the valley spread out below this perch as a white map, broken only by his own trail. He triggered open a ration tube and ate. Of course he could not see the cache from here—but he did hear the broadcast droning through the crisp air.

But it grew monotonous, this staring at the snow and his tracks through it. Diskan wished he did have lenses and could see what lay beyond the tangled wood he had feared to enter. Now and again he watched the sky, once stiffening as a flying thing swooped, until he saw it was no machine but one of the red birds.

As the hours he could not measure wore on, Diskan began to believe his fears of the morning rootless. The voice continued to sound; there was no sign of anyone coming along his trail. There might well be no one but himself of off-world origin on this whole planet. It was cold up here; he might be wasting a whole day to no purpose. Yet he did not want to go back to the cache—not now, anyway. Time enough to return when night closed in. He could do it cleverly, using the same trail back—

It was hard to just sit here, waiting. He studied the part of the valley he could see clearly. It might be wise for him to move along the heights and come up to the cache from another direction. Diskan repacked his supplies into a bag of smaller compress, shouldered the bundle, and began to move, trying to keep to cover, as if he were a Scout moving through enemy territory—though he could not put name to that enemy, nor explain why he was convinced of the need for not revealing his presence.

But he had watchers who knew a kindling of triumph. Their quarry was on the move again—in the right direction.

SEVEN

Diskan must have been on the trail for some time before he saw, beneath the patches of snow and the spotty growth, indications that he was again following a road—not a trail such as animals would make, but one fashioned of blocks of pavement, no longer aligned, yet present. Even in this state, it was easier footing than the cliff edge, and he could make better time, though it struck away at an angle from his course.

The broadcast reached him now as a booming noise in which he could no longer separate the words. And to that, the wind whistling among the rock pillars made a shrill accompaniment.

But the squall that halted him, almost in midstep, was neither voice nor wind. The road entered a cut between two rock spurs, and facing him at the far end of that cut—

Diskan went into a half crouch, his wooden weapon in both hands, the splintered point foremost. The thing was big, much larger than the creature that had accompanied him before. It stood erect, on two stumpy hind legs, so thick with fur that they looked straight. In contrast, its belly was naked and a dull, unhealthy-looking yellow, with small flecks, as if it were coated with scales. Like the scavengers, the creature was, to Diskan's off-world eyes, an unwholesome mixture of animal and reptile.

The head narrowed from a brush of upstanding ragged skin to a snout, where fangs curved up to make a white fringe about yellow lips. But the worst was that it moved forward on its hind legs, its action grotesquely human, its well-armored forepaws raised a little in front of its chest as if it were about to attack him with fists.

That armored snout opened to emit, not the squall Diskan had heard, but a very reptilian hiss, its breath forming a steamy cloud. It was fully his height, or perhaps an inch or so more. And Diskan had no doubt that once within reach of those claws, he had only a slight chance of survival.

Still facing the beast, he withdrew step by step. Luckily, the thing seemed to be in no hurry to close the distance between them. It matched him step by step, and save for the hissing, it gave no sign of active hostility. But he knew he had good reason to fear it.

Back—now he was out of the beginning of the cut, in a place that gave him more room to dodge any rush. He was sure he dared not turn his back and run—such a move would merely bring the enemy to attack. Whether the thing was fast on its feet, he could not tell, but it was fighting in its own territory and had the advantage.

There was space to Diskan's right between two rocks, a narrow slit offering a bolt hole. Diskan backed toward that. The bushy head was sinking between the thing's shoulders. Its hissing climbed to a high note and was almost continuous. It was working itself up to a charge, he was sure.

He was in the crevice now, the wooden spear centered on the beast's midsection. The footing was rough here; he had to glance down now and then to assure himself. And each time he did that, he gave the enemy a second or two of advantage.

Again that other squall. Seemingly out of air a dark body appeared between Diskan and the menace. Back arched, thin tail whipping back and forth in rage, fangs bared, snarling in a rising crescendo of sound, was the furred animal, or one of its kind.

The hissing of the attacker was terrible. And the creature struck with a speed Diskan had not granted its rather clumsy-looking body. Claws curved down, but not into flesh as their owner had intended, for the furred one had dodged with lightning speed, sprung somehow under that blow to strike in turn at the naked yellow belly, opening a spurting slash there. Huge feet stamped, kicked, but the smaller animal had another chance at the big one and opened a second dripping wound.

Only this time it was not so lucky. Claws caught in its fur and swung it off the ground, up to the level of waiting jaws, in spite of its writhing, its flailing paws. Diskan acted. It did not occur to him to leave the two beasts locked in battle, making good his escape. Instead, he leaped forward, his puny weapon ready.

He could not get close to the struggle, but he thrust as true as he could for one of the wide eyes in that head now bending over the fiercely fighting captive. The spear did not go home as he had hoped, but its point raked across the eyeball. The creature gave a fearsome cry and flung up its head.

Diskan stabbed again, trying for a spot beneath that high held head. He had some dim idea that might be a soft place in the creature's body armor. His spear met opposition and did not even penetrate that deceptively naked-looking skin, but the force he had managed to put into the thrust ended the hissing in an explosive grunt.

The beast tried to drop its captive, one paw going to its throat, but the furred one had a hold with teeth and claws about one of the forearms. As the creature kept trying to reach for its throat, its attacker's raking claws scored the flesh of its upper chest with great effectiveness.

The hissing had stopped, but to Diskan's surprise, the snouted head continued to toss in frantic movement. Then it finally tore the furred one loose and threw the animal from it. The heavy furred body struck Diskan, bearing him to the ground.

70

Claws tore his parka but did not reach his skin, as the creature spat, snarled, and strove to free itself from their involuntary entanglement. Moisture spattered Diskan's face—blood from gashes in the furred one's shoulder. It scrambled away from him and turned again to face the enemy with the same hunchbacked stance from which it had launched the battle. But its tail did not whip so swiftly; there were red splotches on the rock beneath it.

The two-footed thing had both paws to its throat, its snout still pointed skyward. It stamped on, not as if hunting them but as though it were trying to escape a torment. Reaching out, Diskan pulled the furred one to him, out of the path of that thing lurching along blindly.

It blundered on past them and was brought up full face against a rock. There it stood for a long moment, its body jerking convulsively, before it went down, its chest heaving, its forepaws beating the air. Diskan relaxed his hold on the other animal. It no longer struggled but lay against him quietly, watching what could only be the dying struggles of the enemy.

But what had killed it? Diskan wiped his hands down the front of his parker. None of the slashes the furred one had inflicted had looked like mortal wounds. And his first blow had not penetrated the eye. He had not even cut the yellow skin when he had aimed at the thing's throat.

Those forepaws now lay limply over the belly; the chest no longer heaved. Diskan thought it must be dead, or close to it.

The furred one got to its feet, giving a little cry of pain when a front paw touched the ground. But it moved in spite of its injuries to the side of the dead thing, sniffing at the upturned snout and then at its throat—as if it, too, were undecided as to what had put an end to the peril.

Diskan retrieved his club-spear before he ventured to approach the body. He had to struggle against revulsion before he could touch that unwholesome corpse.

At the point where his weapon had thudded home on the neck, his fingers found a softened area. Had he by lucky chance broken the thing's windpipe, left it without air to fill its lungs? What mattered most was that it was dead.

The stench rising from the body was such that Diskan drew away and scrubbed his hand in a snow patch to wash from it the feel of the skin he had touched. Then he looked to the furred one.

A deep crimson tongue was licking as far as it could reach along the slash in the animal's shoulder. Another tear bled on its flank. Diskan scooped up snow in both hands and brought it to the injured animal. The steady licking stopped, and those solid, pupil-eyes regarded him. Then the tongue swept out over the snow, back and forth, until it rasped on his palms. He brought more, until it went back to licking its wounds.

Diskan hesitated. Night was coming. He wanted to return to the safety of the cache. Yet he could not walk off and leave the hurt animal here alone. In the freezing night, death could strike. But neither could he carry it across broken country.

A small whine—the furred one was on its feet, gazing at him. And for the second time, Diskan stared into those eyes—to experience once again that odd sense of mixed identity. This was not the same as his contact with the varch, with the beasts of Nyborg, when he had used his projected will to move them to his purposes—and this he did not want! He strove to move his eyes, not to go on into a place where fear ruled.

He began to walk along the ancient road, the furred one limping beside him. Diskan was aware of their movements, but as one who moved in a dream. And he could not break the rhythm of those strides he took. This was a reversal of his usual contact with animals. As the varch had flown to his order, so now he moved to that of the animal beside him.

The battle of wills ended in nothing but exhaustion for Diskan. He retreated in mind even as he obeyed in body. An out-and-out struggle won him nothing. All right, obey—just as he had in the past whenever he saw that rebellion only brought more trouble.

Now and then, as they paused to rest, the animal leaned against Diskan's thigh. Of his own accord, he gripped the loose roll of skin and fur as its shoulders, steadying it whenever it rested so. The tongue-licking appeared to have halted the rush of blood from its wounds, but it moved slowly, in obvious distress.

Together they went through the pass that had been defended by the dead thing. And now the timeworn road descended in a series of wide and shallow steps, cracked and eroded, but not too steep to provide fair footing. Diskan stood at the top, that part of his brain that had retreated from the domination and control of his movements registering what his eyes reported.

Here the spine ridge of the uplands had been cut almost in two by a section of bog running well back. The rim of the cache valley beyond must be a single, almost knife-thin wall, lying now well to his left. The steps of the descent grew wider as they neared the level of the boglands, and from the last step there was only a fall to the water-soaked lowlands. It was late afternoon, but the shadows were not thick enough to veil what stood out in the embrace of the water and mud—square cubes, rectangular blocks of dull black, spaced in a definite design, as if the roofs of some long-drowned city protruded from the grave and engulfed it.

Yet no matter how hard Diskan stared at a building, how he tried to concentrate on its size, its general shape, its position among the rest, there was a queer sensation of not seeing—of an intangible haze between him and the ruins, an unsubstantial aura about it.

Those lines of blocks went on and on, fanning out from the foot of the giant square on which he stood, to vanish well out in the bog. He could not sight the other edge of what must have been an ancient metropolis.

The furred one stood away from him and limped

73

down the first step. Diskan, still under control, followed. This city repelled him, and he struggled to free himself, to return to what now appeared the sanity of the cache.

They halted on that last broad step. Was the furred one intending to leap the last drop, to go out into the morass of sunken buildings? But it settled down with a grunt, lying wounded side up, its eyes on him. Diskan sat down as abruptly, aware that they had reached a journey's end, for the compulsion was gone. He could turn and crawl up the flight of stairs, keep on to the valley of the cache—except that he was too tired, his body aching, his head swimming a little, to try it.

Their present perch was certainly exposed. Snow had drifted across it, and if there was a wind, they could be frozen. He had reached that thought dully when the animal raised its head and looked down into the ruins. There was something so urgent in that movement that Diskan followed its gaze. What was coming had already reached the edge of the platform, a sleek round head there, another, a third—

They climbed up, balanced on their haunches, eying their fellow and then Diskan with those compelling, unwinking stares. Soundless communication? One of the trio advanced and squatted down beside the wounded one, its head moving back and forth as if by sense of smell it examined the slashes. Then it set to licking the wounds.

The other two vanished with that flashing speed Diskan had seen his companion use in battle. He had brought the creature to the aid of its own kind; they or it had released him. He could no longer question the fact of their intelligence. However, their interest in him had preceded the fight in the pass. Could it have been that the wounded one had deliberately entered into that battle on his behalf?

Diskan watched the two with dull wonder. He could see no difference in them as to size or color or fur. They might have been twins of one birth. The wounded one gave the impression of now resting at ease, confident that its comrade's attention would restore it.

A flicker at the edge of the platform, a head rising. In the sharp-toothed jaws of the newcomer were sticks, several of them. The animal crossed the stone and dropped its burden not far from the man. And it was not alone—two more, carrying gleanings from the swamp edge, followed. And they came and went, adding to the pile.

Diskan was past wonder now. He brought the offerings to a place not far from the wounded animal and built a fire. Miraculously, though he was not impressed by such miracles anymore, his fire stone still held life. And the flames arose as the wood gatherers continued to appear with more fuel.

He opened his bag of rations. To offer its contents to the busy furred ones would be to exhaust his provisions in perhaps one meal, but he hesitated as he picked out a tube, glancing at the wounded one. His concern was unnecessary. A head, held high because of a wriggling silver thing gripped in the mouth, appeared in the firelight. The captive was tossed down before the patient, who, with a thump of the paw, stilled the offering and then proceeded to dine.

Diskan ate, fed the fire, and watched the comings and goings of the furred ones. Since he could not identify individuals and they moved on and off the platform so constantly, he could not tell how many there were. The one who had come to nurse the wounded one remained, crouched beside its patient, now and again licking the slashes, while the others came and went, some singly and some in twos and threes.

With food in him and the warmth of the fire thawing out his numbed body, Diskan began to feel stronger. Testing his companions, he went to the stairs, ascended a step or two. They paid him no more than passing attention. He was certain he could leave if he willed. But why do so now? He had fire—and they were still bringing fuel, as if to feed it all night long. They had made no hostile move.

And—Diskan realized suddenly—he did not want to leave—to leave them! He had been alone since the ship spat him forth in that final attempt to save his life—except for the visits of the furred one or ones. Once he had wanted to be alone, away from the pity and rejection of his own kind. But here—here he could not turn his back on the fire and the animals and strike out into the twilight merely to hunt the cache, which was a deserted shelter for his own species.

Diskan hurried back to the fire. His boot struck something lying beneath the snow and sent the object flying into the full light of the flames, where it glistened. He picked it up.

A stunner! He stared down at the weapon in disbelief. Meant to temporarily paralyze, not to kill, but secondary weapon of all spacemen, it was the weapon he had hoped to find in the cache, not here on the open rock. This was a precious find. Diskan quickly read the charge dial. It was half expended, if the guage was to be believed. So this had been fired, and then dropped—

From the weapon, he glanced at the animals. Had it been fired at them? They had not seemed hostile. But there could be reasons for their apparent harmlessness. Now he had a weapon far more effective than his club-spear.

Diskan hunkered down closer to the fire, searching the butt of the stunner for any mark of ownership, but it was discouragingly bare—just ordinary issue. Another trace of the cache people?

He turned to where he had found it, kicking loose the snow. Nothing else, and the weapon could have lain there for days—months. Carefully he put it inside his parka, so it rested heavy and cold against his middle, his confidence growing from that weight.

Once more he settled beside the fire, sleep pulling at him. The wounded furred one and its nurse had curled up together, and the others had disappeared. Diskan's head nodded. He pulled out the stunner, and curled his fingers around it as he lay down.

76

He watched the fire drowsily, hardly conscious of movement to his left. It was just another fuel carrier, bringing bigger branches this time. Odd color about them—leaves—the frozen leaves of the wood in the lake valley—red leaves—

And the animal—it was feeding the fire, pushing those leafed branches straight into the heart of the blaze. Diskan tried to rouse, but he was too sleepy—far too sleepy.

EIGHT

Xcothal— Diskan walked through water, sweet, ever-flowing water, sometimes calf high, sometimes, when he came to an intersection of streets, knee high. There was a scent to the water, fresh, sharp, astringent, very good in his nostrils. Xcothal at feast time. But he could only see dimly as if he moved in a dream—and he wanted to see it clearly, all the beauty and light and color!

Around him splashed and romped the brothers-in-fur, the companion ones, as eager as he for the feasting and playtime to come. Their thoughts sometimes meshed with his, so that he savored the pleasure of the water paths, saw and felt as he would not see and feel by means of his own body. This was Xcothal the great, and he was moving to its heart where a wonder beyond all wonders waited.

But the others—not the brothers—the others? There were shadows; yes, he caught glimpses of them, never long enough to give them substance, bone, and flesh—to make them real. And Xcothal was not a deserted city. It held life other than his within its walls, its streets, which were brooks and streams. He wanted to meet that life, be one with it, with a longing so intense that it was a pain! Yet though he turned and watched, there were only shadows.

Carven faces on the walls, runes running. Those he could almost read and knew, in his failure, that had he been able to read them rightly, the shadows would be substance. Always so close, always to fail!

Yet the brothers-in-fur were not shadows, and that thought sustained Diskan to try and try again. Perhaps when he reached the wonder, then it would all come right. But that was so far! He walked through the water; the buildings passed him on either hand, too blurred for him to be truly sure of their form, knowing somehow that he could never enter them even if he turned aside from this street.

His first mind-filling joy was fading as the pain of longing and loneliness grew sharper. The brothers-in-fur, they knew. They had ceased their play, had come to him and pressed against him now and then reassuringly, the touch of their damp fur a caress. But he knew—knew now—that this was not the true Xcothal. This was but a dream, though it might be a way-dream sent to him for a purpose. And in his eyes tears stung for a loss that grew heavier as he went on and on through a shadow Xcothal in search of shadows—an endless quest.

Dawn made the sky a silver bowl. The fire still smoldered in a circle of dark forms on the stone platform above the swamp. Diskan moaned and flung out an arm, as if he tried to grasp something that was fast fading from him. There were tear stains on his cheeks. His eyes were still closed. About him those others stirred, got to their haunches, all facing the fire.

So far he has gone.

It is not enough! Sharply impatient.

Do not hurry this. Would you lose all by haste?

He is like the other one—the female. So far but not enough.

Perhaps. But it can be that the Place will unlock the door.

Never enough. Sadness, misery of loss.

We shall not put aside trying. Let him wake now. Put on him the wish; let him seek that which must be found, in his body this time.

That way is dangerous; there are the swamp traps.

So? Are we not here to watch and direct? The female and the others, they walked in safely, did they not? And this one is certainly not less than them. Perhaps he is more, much more. Wake him; set on him the wish; follow where he cannot see us. Is this agreed?

Seconds of silence and then: *Agreed.*

Diskan opened his eyes and looked up at the sky. The enchantment of the dream still held him. He expected to see the color of those buildings and to feel the softness of the air that had enfolded him as he walked the streets of water, not this chill and austere sky. Then the dream powdered into nothingness and he sat up.

The fire was there and by it still a few sticks, but the animals that had shared its warmth were gone, even the wounded one. He sat alone, looking out over the dark ruins.

"Xcothal," he said aloud. That was Xcothal, or what Xcothal had become with the dimming power of many centuries pressing it down into a rising tide of mud and water. Somewhere, in the heart of that waste, was what he must find. He went to the edge of the platform to look at the frozen swampland. Patches of dull blue, breaking the surface of the ways between the blocks of the buildings, warned of mud holes. Not an easy road, but the one he must follow.

Diskan ate, checked the stunner, picked up his bag of supplies and the club-spear. Then he jumped from the platform to the level of the city.

There was a sharp cry; birds wheeled up from roosting space on the roof of the nearest building. They were white and black, the colors sharply contrasted. Now they skimmed ahead of him, uttering their cries to alert the silent city against an intruder come to disturb its drugged sleep.

Diskan picked his way with care. Frozen and dried vegetation was his guide from step to step, with now and then the solid footing of some stone blocks tumbled from their original settings. But, where in his dream he had been upheld by a sense of joyful excitement, now he traveled in a somber cloud of uneasiness and with the feeling of loss.

Doorways gaped at him, opening upon dark interiors. He had no desire to explore any of them. On the walls were faint traces, much worn, of the carvings he remembered, and even more obscured lines, which could be the runes he had wanted so to read.

Brothers-in-fur—the animals that had gamboled beside him on that other walk through Xcothal—Diskan kept watching for them. But no paw print, no glimpse of a dark body, gave him companionship now. He glanced back once, to see that the shoreline, marked by the steps, was well behind. Then the street curved to the right, and a building hid them from view.

Pools of water, even though roofed with ice, slowed him while he found a way about them. Luckily, the blue mud holes were few along this street, and both times he had come to them, there had been room at one side for passing. It was when Diskan paused by a fallen wall to scoop up some of the snow to allay his thirst that he saw the first indication that there might be other life within that dreary waste.

Ice had been broken at the edge of a pool, and in the mud of its verge were prints, frozen iron hard now. Diskan bent over them.

"Boots!" He identified the marks aloud and then started as the word echoed hollowly back to him. But those were boot prints right enough and beyond them another mark, as if the maker had fallen and braced his weight on his hands to rise again. A hand print—the five fingers well defined in the mud. But a small hand—Diskan set his own down beside the mark for comparison. A hand print, and boot impressions, and the stunner he had found. Some off-worlder had come this way before him. And judging by the size of the hand print—a small off-worlder.

Diskan set a brisker pace. A single man lost, disarmed? There was nothing to fear from him, and perhaps it meant company in his desolate place. Perhaps a shout might bring the stranger? Yet Diskan hesitated. He shrank from arousing the sullen echoes. A shout could be a cry to end the world.

Now why had he thought that? To end the world— how *had* the world of Xcothal ended? In that dream, he had seen the city in its glory and power—now he wandered through it dead, with the signs of great age upon it. There were centuries, maybe even thousands of planet years, between that "then" and this "now." Yet, the brothers-in-fur had existed then, and they had certainly been with him in the now— unless they were an illusion, too.

Diskan shivered. Of what could he be sure? Never before had he been forced to look outside himself and guess what was real and what was not, because he had been only too well aware of the real, and that for him was ever present with pressure and rejection. Vaanchard had been real, Nyborg had been real, and the crèche had been real. But here the real and the unreal flowed together. He could stamp his foot on the frozen mud, feel the jar of that contact throughout his body, thus making sure of the truth of where he stood. But last night he had been as sure of the soft water about his legs—in these same streets.

And he had traveled with the furred ones in both the real and the unreal, so how could he be sure of either any more? Perhaps today was also a dream— perhaps Diskan Fentress lay encased in the mud-filled spacer. He jerked away from that path of thought. No—for the second time he stamped. *This* was real! This was now and it was real. And, judging by those tracks, another of his kind had found it real before him.

He set out again, down the street that no longer ran straight but curved. And as he went, he watched for any signs of the one who had gone that way before him. The size of the city began to impress him. He had been walking at a steady pace for a considerable time, and still the street continued to stretch on and on with only one change—the buildings were growing higher as he advanced. Where none had been more than two stories tall when he had entered the city, now they were double that, and fewer had broken walls. Ahead, he could sight still higher erections. The blue mud patches had vanished, and the coarse mats of brittle grass and vegetation were thicker. Now and again Diskan saw the black and white birds perched on the upper windowsills watching him inquisitively. They must accept him now as harmless, for they no longer flew ahead cawing a warning.

However, the very fact that the birds were quiet nibbled at his nerves. Save that they did move, sidling along their perches, they could be less-worn carvings to ornament the dead city. Diskan glanced up at them now and then. They had an attitude of interest, showing no fear but rather confidence that whatever was about to happen would not involve them.

What was about to happen? That expectancy was a part of it all, a waiting growing in intensity, willing him to do something, be somewhere.

The day was dull and cloudy, though there was no more snow. Perhaps the sun could have made the canyon between buildings less dour. Deliberately, Diskan halted, dropping his supply bag, seating himself on some steps leading up to a doorway with a sense of defiance. He ate, slowly, drawing out the meal as long as possible, His vision of Xcothal, which had lingered beyond the dream, had worn away during the day, as if he had rubbed it off against these age-old stones. As he gazed about him now, he wondered how he could ever believe this city had been alive.

And who had lived here then? Those shadows that had remained shadows with no definite shape? Why—it could just as well have been dead in his dream or at least uninhabited, save for the brothers-in-fur—

A sound, echoing. Diskan's hand went to the stunner, but he did not draw that weapon. A limping paw had dislodged a stone to announce the coming of the one who now moved to meet him, for this was the one who had fought in the road pass.

And the eyes were on Diskan. He shrugged and picked up his supply bag. There was no reason for him to fight that summons, one he felt was imperative. He moved on, his dream reviving as the brother-in-fur limped beside him. There were others, too. Diskan did not need to see them. Their presence was as tangible as if he could lay hand on their fur.

On and on, the buildings always rising. The city, speculated Diskan, must be not unlike a pyramid. Odd that he had not noticed that fact from the ridge top on his first sighting of the ruins. He could now count more than ten stories before the weathered and broken rooflines showed. But ahead was a yet taller building.

This was it, the place he strove to reach in the dream! Why he was sure of that, he could not tell, but he was. They came out in the open, into a square, or rather a circle, into which fed street after street, as the spokes of a wheel might join the hub. The center-most building was unlike the rest in that it, too, was round, a stairway encircling it, to lead to a covered arcade. Diskan crossed the open and began to climb the stair.

Now those who had accompanied him unseen were in the open, following him in a dark pack, soundless in their pacing, keeping always a little to the rear, in numbers he could not reckon.

The arcade presented him with a choice of doors. Diskan took the nearest and stepped into a gloom so great that he was blinded for those moments it took his eyes to adjust. Then a thin filter of light from above showed him that he stood in a wedge-shaped room, narrowing at the far end. That was all, bare walls, bare floor, nothing!

He looked to the one who had limped beside him.

"What do you want?" he demanded, and his words echoed.

They wanted something of him, and that demand for action unknown battered him. He must *do* something—perform some act they were waiting for. Only they gave him no clue, and the tension built in him until he cried aloud:

"I don't know what you want! Can't you understand? I don't *know!*"

The shout relieved some of the pressure, or were they releasing him from the burden of their need? There was a stir. Diskan glanced over his shoulder. As silently as they had come in his wake, they were retreating, leaving him here alone. Alone! He could not bear being alone—not here!

Diskan dropped his supply bag, his club-spear.

"No—!" He was on his knees, reaching for the limping one with more than entreaty, a determination that, come what might, he would keep that one with him.

There was angry hissing—eyes blazing into his, a rejection so utter and complete that it froze Diskan until the animal had limped out of range. Then that one, too, was gone, and he was alone.

All the pressure he had half sensed since the morning's awaking was off him, but the void it left was so frightening that Diskan could not find the strength to move. Something great and wonderful, without description in any words of his, had been waiting here. And through his own stupidity it was lost. Logic told him that was not true, but emotion hammered back it was—it *was!*

He was reaching for his club when he saw some marks in the dust on the floor, for the longer he sat there, the more his sight increased. Not clear prints—but someone, or something, had been there before him. Dully, for the want of a better purpose, he began to follow them.

Outside once again, in the covered way to which the steps led. Soil had blown in here through the centuries. There were clumps of withered grass rooted in the larger deposits. And the tracks—much sharper now—boots! Two pairs, maybe three—and a place where another had trod across that trail. Three—

four others here! With a chance, they might still be!

Diskan broke into a shambling trot. The trail circled the building to another doorway. He hesitated by that. Night was almost here. He had no liking for the interior of the building in the dark. What memories, what ghosts could walk here in a man's dreams? He dared not dream again of Xcothal as it had been.

But there was light beyond, a thin diffused gleam that came from no visible opening. It might have been born from the air itself. There were tracks leading straight across the rooms. Mechanically, Diskan followed them, to be confronted by a bare wall into which they vanished.

Shaken, he put his hand to the blocking surface. It moved, so easily that he went off balance and fell into a corridor, also dimly lit. Here the dust had not gathered so thickly; there was only a smudge or two to point the trail. And the corridor was circular, apparently following the line of the outer wall.

Diskan took to thumping the wall on his left, seeking another of those masked openings. His guess was proved right when a second swinging stone moved, and he looked into a well-like space. Up and down that curled a stair. Down he would not go—the gloom hung there. But up—from the floor above he might have a full view of the city and learn where he now was in relation to the swamp shore from which he had come. Diskan climbed, not finding it easy, for the steps were steep and narrow, and there appeared to be no more openings or landings until he came to the top.

He felt his way about that space, with no idea how far he now was above street level. Another door stone opened into a much wider corridor, its right wall broken by arches through which he could look into the clouded evening sky. Wind blew in freshly, and Diskan went to stand there.

The city spread out below; yet between him and those buildings and streets, there was a curious haze, not a fog or mist such as he knew elsewhere, but more a distortion of sight, so that one moment a building could look so, the next seem altogether different. Diskan was forcibly reminded of Xcothal as he had seen it in his dream. There was no color, none of the feeling of happy rightness; yet the Xcothal he surveyed from this perch was not the ruined city.

That distortion did not frighten him; on the contrary, it soothed the sense of loss that had ridden him since his failure to fulfill the plan of the brothers-in-fur. Diskan continued to watch the shifting scenes below until a vast fatigue weighted his eyes and he shuffled back, to drop with his shoulders the inner wall, his hands resting on his knees. His eyes closed. Dream—he was willing to dream again. Perhaps he would find the answer so.

But tonight there were no dreams.

Shadows flitted through the streets, held council together.

He is not to our purpose—as the others were not. Forget him.

Yet he dreamed clearly. Of the others, only the female dreamed, and as she dreamed, she feared, awaking to call on the powers of her own kind for protection. He dreamed, and in his dreams he was happy; thus he is unlike the others.

Have you thought this, wise ones? We may not again find what once we had, but this one could be shaped to our purposes?

A hard task shaping. And in the process of shaping, that which is shaped may break.

Yet let that not deter the shaping. How think you, one and all?

Long has been the waiting—we are only half of the whole. This one has been the most responsive yet. Let shaping be tried. Do we agree thus?

We agree.

Diskan slept soundly as the shadows separated and went to accomplish purposes of their own in the streets of Xcothal.

NINE

The black and white birds wheeled and circled outside the arched openings. Diskan watched them apathetically. He had not moved from the place that night and fatigue had chosen for his rest, though the sun was bright and the day sky cleared of all clouds. He felt emptied, without any wish to move, to think, to be—

But now life sparked within him. Dragging himself to his feet, Diskan walked slowly back to the stair that had brought him to this perch above the city. Wearily, he circled down, around and around that spiral, slowly, as the descent made him dizzy. There was a great silence within the walls of the building. Was it a temple, a fortress, a palace? One of three—or all—he would never be sure.

Diskan came out in the lower hall. Now much plainer to read were the tracks he had followed the night before. For want of any other employment, he began to trace again those others' passing.

Shoulder high on one wall—a blackened streak. No stunner left that! Blaster raying, though he was not too familiar with the traces of those lethal weapons. And just beyond that scar a door stood open. Diskan drew his stunner. Against a blaster that was hardly better than the club-spear, but it was the best he had.

The room beyond startled him. In this building he had seen no signs of ruin and decay, but now he fronted walls that were holed, riven in great gaps, with a crumble of debris out on the floor of the chamber. And each of those holes gave upon blackness, as if there were great open space beyond.

Fire marks—sears of blast. This chaos, Diskan realized, was not the result of time, but the work of man, energetically tearing into fabric of the building—searching for what? He began a cautious circuit of the chamber, detouring about the rubble, longing for a lamp with which to explore the darkness beyond.

A chattering. Diskan swung the stunner, thumbed the button, and saw a mass collapse limply. He turned over with the toe of his boot the body of one of the scavengers such as he had seen at the burned ground.

He stopped near some claw-marked stone, from under which came a dark oozing, now dried. Diskan dropped his supply bag to examine the fall of stone more carefully. Gingerly, he began to lever the top of the mass apart, then leaped away as it cascaded from him into the gap of the broken wall.

Sound reached him from the shaking mound, a clicking. Diskan readied the stunner, watching for another of the scavengers, but the limited light revealed instead a head, shoulders, an outflung arm. The man was dead, had been so for some time. What Diskan could see of his clothing suggested a spacer uniform, and there was the glint of an officer's insignia on his upstanding collar.

On the wrist of the outflung arm was a wide bracelet inset with a dial. The face of that glowed, and from it came a steady ticking—a com device of some sort. And it was recording or broadcasting—or whatever—even now. On impulse, Diskan pulled the thing over the cold hand and brought it into better light.

A dial, without any sumbols or figures he could read, only a single needle that swayed as he moved the bracelet, swinging so that its delicately arrowed head always pointed in the same direction, to his right now, but ever to one wall as he tested it by turning. A direction finder of sorts. Intrigued, Diskan tried to slip it over his own wrist, discovered the supporting ring too small, and finally attached it to his belt.

He returned to the dead man. Two blocks Diskan could not move imprisoned the body, but he cleared away enough of the rubble to see what had brought the man down. Not the fall of the wall, which had partly entombed him, but a blaster burn across his body breast high. The condition of the chamber was now clear; it had been a battlefield. Slowly, Diskan piled the largest stones he could find back over what he had uncovered for the only burial he could give the stranger.

Now he wanted to get out into the light of day. He struck at the limp scavenger with the club before he left, thus making sure it would not return to its digging. As he went, Diskan watched the device he had taken from the body.

The needle still pointed in one direction, and it seemed to Diskan that the clicking accelerated. What could it be attuned to? Others roaming this pile, carrying on some desperate struggle of their own? Diskan had no wish to be involved. But still the swing of the needle intrigued him, and he followed its lead along the outer corridor.

Then that hair-thin guide pointed left. Diskan searched the wall for an entrance, and the stone gave under his hand. Before him was a hole blasted in the surface of the far wall. The clicking was a steady purr, but that purr warned him. He had no wish to walk into blaster fire. Slowly, Diskan backed away and let the outer door slide into place behind him. This was another mystery of Xcothal and one *he* did not want to solve.

Walking firmly, he went out of the building into which the animals had brought him. When he was on the stairs in the outer air, he breathed deeply. He must get away, free himself from the dead city, from his failure here. The quarrel of off-world strangers was none of his. He felt a curious detachment, as if he had no tie with his own species any more.

He had drawn heavily on his supplies. Could he work his way back to the cache? Diskan closed his eyes for the moment, trying mentally to picture the route he had come. It was simple. He might not be trained to track, but there was nothing difficult about this. He strode confidently down the stairs and looked for the opening into the street that had brought him here.

Then his confidence ebbed a little. All those wheel spokes of open ways looked exactly alike. He had come in there—no, there—or had he? He could not tell by the buildings; they were all the same.

The morning's sun had melted the snow patches that might have held tracks; he had no guide save chance. But that was the way to the ridge. Diskan turned to face it. And surely, once pointed in the right general direction, he could find his way. Let him see the ridge as a landmark and he was safe.

He entered the street he had chosen. Too bad he had not been more observant yesterday. But during the last part of that journey, after the animal had joined him, he had been aware only of his companions, the one beside him and those he could not see. And of those, there had been no trace since they had left him in the wedge chambers.

If this was not the street he had traversed yesterday, it was very like it. The sun glistened on what Diskan thought was a runnel of ice and then saw was a track, a shining mark running straight from one building to another. He poked at it with the spear point, and the wood skidded on a slick, slimy surface, rising with a ball of noxious material on its tip. Diskan thrust it again and again into a hummock of grass to clean it. He hurried on, not liking the looks of that trail, if trail it was, and certainly not wishing to investigate its source.

The birds and the animals had been in the city yesterday, but now he began to see disturbing traces of other possible inhabitants. A second slime trail, wider, thicker, and more disgusting than the first crossed the street. And this time Diskan had to take a running leap to clear it. Perhaps the creatures who made these were night crawlers. If so, the sooner he won out of the city, the better. It had lost for him all the appeal of his dream; its sinister aspect was growing, so that even when the sun shone brightly into its streets, the buildings seemed to exhale gloom from their open doorways, setting up a fog of fear.

Diskan broke into a trot, glancing from side to side, and now and then over his shoulder. There was no movement, no sight of anything. But that very stillness was part of his discomfort, for it hinted at things lying in wait behind a window, within the shadow of a doorway. Allowing him to come, to pass, then following— Twice he stopped short, faced about, stunner ready, certain that he *had* heard some betraying noise, that danger prowled at his heels.

He consulted the device he had taken from the dead man. The clicking was very faint, barely audible when he held it to his ear. And the needle pointed back to the center of the city. He was sure the peril he sensed had nothing to do with his own kind. This was of the city, yet not of Xcothal. An empty shell had been left, and into that emptiness had crawled other things that had no kinship with those who had built the shell, who were, in fact, the opposite of those first intelligences. This was no city of promised light, color, and joy, as he had seen it yesterday, but a graveyard, given over to all that opposed his dream.

More slime tracks, and one so wide that he feared he could not leap it. The noisome odor was stronger; the tracks could perhaps be fresher. Then Diskan knew that he had chosen the wrong road, for the street widened into a great pool with a center of blue mud. And that mud blew a bubble as he watched, the dull skin swelling out and out—to break, spewing bits of yellow stuff over the surface of the lake.

The yellow substance was light enough to be airborne, floating in motes. Some of these sped together as steel attracted to a magnet. And when they met,
92

there was a spark of fire, a small flaming coal, which fell to melt a bit of ice or set flame to a tuft of dried reed. And there was a stench worse than that from the slime tracks.

No safe way of crossing that lake. The ice crust was thin, and Diskan did not trust the footing along its shore, which lapped against the walls of the buildings. Back—back to the hub circle and choose again, and Diskan had the feeling that something was satisfied, amused by his retreat.

At the circle, he sat down on one of the steps of the center building. Here the sun shown warmer, more brightly. When he looked down any one of those streets, it was to meet obscurity, akin to that which had bewildered him when he had surveyed the city from the arched walk at the top of the tower structure. Yet this was different, for then he had a sense of expectant enchantment, whereas this warned, repelled, set up a barrier. Diskan weighed the bag of supplies. He could ration what was left. All these supplies carried various sustaining ingredients that allowed one to stretch them thin and still have an adequate level of nourishment. But he wanted out—away from those now-sinister streets, back to the natural rock and marsh he could understand.

Deliberately, he studied the four streets to his left. Down the first he had just returned. But he had retained enough memory of yesterday to limit the possible exit to one of those four—or the three he had not tried. Now he selected the center one of the trio and set out for the second time.

Slime trails again, but these had hardened in the frosty air. For the rest, this way was exactly like the first.

He held to a brisk walk. It was past midday, and he wanted to be out of this maze before sundown. To be caught at night in one of these dark ways was a risk he did not want to take, and he must make good time now.

A lake, with blue mud for its center— Diskan did

93

not believe what he saw. He rammed the spear point against the ice surface at his feet, and it pierced the pane over dark fluid, releasing an evil smell, proving its reality. He was back again! But he had not taken the same street—he could not have made that mistake!

Holding fiercely to that belief, Diskan retreated for the second time. The street that had brought him here before—that had been the first of those probable ones, and this had been the third! He knew that was true. Yet as far as he could see, he stood now just where he had before—

Back to the hub. Panting and sweating, he squatted once again on the steps and counted those streets with a finger. He had been right! Here was the ration tube he had sucked dry and left lying to mark where he had rested. *That* was the first street, *that* the third! And since they radiated out spokewise, why, one could not run into the other without some curve he would have noticed. Yet he had found the lake the second time.

Diskan put his head in his hands and tried to consider the problem carefully, logically, only there was no normal logic in this. So, he must have counted wrong some way. Only he had not, one part of his brain shrieked—he had *not!* This was the old frustration, the old defeating knowledge that somehow he had not performed some function with the right responses. Thoroughly shaken, Diskan was almost afraid now to lift his head and look at those streets so much alike, so much a trap for him.

When he did raise his eyes to survey them with a control he fought to hold, the obscurity had deepened. Why, he was hardly able to see down any length farther than the first three or four buildings. Diskan gave a gasping cry, caught up supply bag and club, and began to climb the steps of the core building. For all his determination, he could *not* face the murk of those streets. And to come a third time to that lake would be more than his sanity could stand.

He pushed in the first open door and looked about

the deep gloom of the hall into which the animals had brought him. Full circle! It must have been near this same hour yesterday that he had stood here. Then he had been keyed to desires, pressures from without. Now he was alone—very much alone.

Diskan gazed at the blank walls, his eyes always returning to the point of the wedge where the dusk was thickest. Yet he had no uneasiness of spirit such as had frightened him in the somberness of the streets. What had been the purpose of this chamber? It was so large, companies of worshipers could have gathered here. Was it a fane? Or hundreds of councilors could have debated together if this was a place of government. A court might have held vast formal ceremonials down its length. Now all was silence, dust, shadows. No trace of carving, no matter how worn, none of the vague impressions of what might be runes ran along the smooth surfaces of the narrowing walls, no altar, no dais, no throne raised from the floor.

He began to walk toward the narrowed point. At his belt, the device ticked more and more loudly. His glance told him that the needle pointed ahead when he held it on his palm. But here was no rubble or battle sign.

Suddenly, Diskan spoke. "What do you want of me?"

In a measure he had begun to feel as he had the day before—that a demand was building, becoming more imperative, that he was being given a second chance at some test, the importance of which was past his assessing.

He was midway down the chamber now. Did the shadows gathered at the point have substance? Were the animals returning? No, he could not see them, turning, pacing, moving in to meet him. Nothing so concrete awaited him. Still some sense tricked him, or his eyes, into that belief in movement, in the appearance of a pattern forming there, woven to a purpose he could not guess. If he could only follow the lines of that pattern, he might understand! But though he concentrated, tried to force such understanding, it did

95

not come—only that movement he could not trace. And at last it dwindled into nothingness and was gone.

"*Tell me!*" His voice arose in a despairing cry, echoing through the hall. But when those echoes died away, there was only a dusty silence and a loss that hurt.

Diskan waited, hoping to see again that weaving which was only half on the borderline of his sight, to catch from the air about him some helpful hint of purpose, to learn the step to be taken, the unseen door that must be opened. Nothing— Whatever had brought a small measure of life for a portion of time to this age-old hall had died, as a fire might fall to ashes, its flames unfed.

He turned at last, his shoulders hunched and bowed, his pace a tired shuffle. This last and perhaps greatest of his failures left him drained of all purpose and feeling. He went out to the hall, and because he had no place else to go, he found again the inner stair and climbed to his perch of the night before. Below was Xcothal, but this time he had no desire to look out upon its ruins. He feared what he might see in those streets as the night closed in.

As one who nurses a pain that cannot be soothed, he rocked slowly back and forth on his haunches, his arms folded over his middle.

"What do you want of me?" That was no shout, only a ragged whisper, but he repeated it over and over, until his mouth was dry, his voice husky. And there was never any answer, not even the cry of a bird.

He did not sleep; he could not. The sense of danger arose about his post as the fumes of the mud lake had billowed up with their choking stench. No test of courage could be harder to face. In the darkness, Diskan fought back, and he had so little to fight with! But the hour came when, because he could not live with his own fear any longer, Diskan crawled on hands and knees across the cold stone to look down on the city, the pit from which that terror arose.

Dark such as he had not imagined—yet the longer

he watched, the more he saw that there were degrees of darkness in a way he could find no words to describe. There was a flowing, an ebbing there also—not to be defined—a life that was not his life, nor the life of that other weaving in the chamber. This was a thing that had entered unbidden, that strove to knit itself into the ruined walls, to remain, unless that which had once been came again.

That which had once been! Xcothal—

"It is past—" He did not know why he spoke that protest in a frozen whisper.

Past! Past! Perhaps his word had been taken up by an echo; perhaps it was only the sigh of a breeze below his lookout. The coiling of the dark upon the dark grew swifter, reached higher about the hub building. Diskan made himself watch it. His body shivered and his nails cut deeper into his own flesh, although he was not aware of that small pain through the larger that filled him.

Xcothal—he clung to his dream, strove to batter aside the tide of darkness with the color, the life, the beauty it smothered and buried. Xcothal should not be taken! That which had dwelt here could not be so lightly overcome, banished— Xcothal— Diskan stared into the night and fought—throwing away all logic, all reason.

He only knew that, in summoning his dream and holding it, he was waging a small engagement in the midst of a battle, and he held to his post grimly. What had been dark waves beating on shadows began to change. He did not know when he saw that first spark of light flash into being, a pinpoint in the streets. But there came another and another—minute sparks of light whose origin he could not guess. They followed no pattern, a cluster here, a line of individual points there, a solitary beam in the midst of heavy dusk.

They did not move as did the whirling lashings of the dark but endured as outposts. And at length, no more appeared. Diskan unclenched his fists. Again on his hands and knees, he went back to the wall. He did not want to sleep; he did not need it. There was a tingling awareness of the night, such as he had never experienced before, running through his veins, warming him so that with impatient fingers he pulled at the throat of the parka, opening it farther.

Something—he did not know just what—had happened, as if a machine long idle had been triggered into action once again, and ripples spreading from that action were lapping on, out and out. Was this what they had wanted of him, the brothers-in-fur? No, swift on the heels of that came the denial, and he knew it was the truth. He had failed then, but now—

Diskan did not notice the device hung at his belt. On the dial the needle quivered, fluttered; the clicking was a solid purr that did not reach his deaf ears. All that was real for him now was what lay out there in the night, stirring, moving. And this time—surely this time—he was going to learn what it was!

TEN

Not a sound but a vibration in the air, through his body, was transmitted by the stone on which he crouched. A summons? After it, a quiver, as if each and every heavy stone in these walls strove to answer, only had no way of giving voice. Diskan waited tense, yearning—

Again!

His body obeyed without any command from *his* brain as he stood up. In his veins, the blood flowed more quickly; he felt alert, ready for anything that might come. The deadening fog of fear had been rent into tatters, was shriveling from him.

In the dark, needing no physical sight as a guide, Diskan found the stairs, began to descend. Beat—once again! A heart awakening into life—Xcothal's heart? In his eagerness, he stumbled, almost fell, and that mishap taught him caution. Round and around, down, always waiting for that beat of life within the core of ancient death.

He was on the threshold of the wedge-shaped chamber when it vibrated for the fourth time. And he saw the furred ones moving up the steps, slipping around and about him, as if he had no existence in their eyes. There was no reckoning the number of their dark shapes in this pale light. Diskan only knew that they were many and that they came from all directions, pressing with purpose up the outer steps, toward the wedge chamber. The brothers-in-fur! But they could not be alone—there must be the others!

Bewildered, Diskan drew to one side just within the doorway, his eyes searching for what he felt must be there, though what he sought, he could not explain. The interior of the huge hall, which had been so dusky, was now growing lighter. Sparks hung in the air here and there, always above the mass of furred bodies, reared up on their broad haunches, their heads all turned to the narrow far end, as if fixed in a hypnotic stare on some point or thing *he* could not see. There were so many of them!

Now their heads moved, a rhythmic ripple that ran back like a breaking wave to Diskan's place by the door. And following that ripple came the vibration, stronger now, a beat that shook the building, the living things in it, as if the very earth heaved.

Ripple, ripple. With a start, Diskan became conscious his own head had joined in the slow bend forward and back. The sparks in the air grew brighter. They were of different colors, gems tossed aloft to hang in brilliant array—green, blue, orange, scarlet, violet, shades in between, dazzling to watch.

From over the heads of the animals, the lights moved out and away, drifting to the bare walls. But where they touched the stone they melted, spread in glistening runnels and shooting trails of jeweled fire. And they were not still, those runnels and trails, but moved, interweaving, loosing, weaving again another design, as had the dusky shadows. Only this was the splendor of which that had been the dying ashes.

Diskan shaded his eyes with his hand from what was close to searing brilliance. He longed to watch, and yet he could no longer do so. He was on his knees, his head moving in time with those of the animals about him. And from them, a vast wave of ecstasy, which was also expectancy of some greater wonder to come, rose about him.

Boom! Boom! Xcothal awakening—the past returning to flower again.

100

Yes! Yes! Diskan's lips shaped the words he could not voice aloud. To know—to be in Xcothal in this hour! This was what he had sought without understanding. He stood on a threshold; take only one step and wonder beyond reckoning was his!

A scream—

The fabric of lights, of rapport with the animals, was rent as if a knife had slashed it. Dazed, Diskan shook and shivered. He fell forward, and that saved his life, for over him a blaster volt blazed, to strike the wall and scar it with a core of crimson destruction.

Diskan twisted, still too much under the spell to know more than that it had been broken. He stared up, bemused, at the smoking evidence of that shot. Then he was knocked down and rolled over by furred bodies launched at him. And by the time he fought his way free of those, his wits were back.

Had he really been attacked by the animals? Diskan thought not as he sat up, back against the wall, well out of line of the doorway from which that blast must have come. His companions in that ritual had merely removed him speedily from the line of fire.

Fire from an off-world weapon! Now a piercing buzzing from his belt! Had the device guided the enemy here? Diskan unhooked it and almost threw it from him, his grief and anger at the interruption turning into a smoldering rage. No, he would hunt that other down! He had been close to dying in that ray, yes. But what was worse, he had lost that which had been almost within his grasp here. And for that there was no pardon! This thing he held in his hand, it could perhaps guide him to his attacker.

However, as he scrambled up, the animals pressed about him, imposed their bodies as a barrier between him and the doorway.

"No!" Diskan strove to elude their guard. "Let me through!" He thrust against them. Then he remembered the stunner, dragged it out, and sprayed widely with it.

That cleared a path as the animals went down,

101

temporarily paralyzed. Diskan ran into the night, the com device in one hand, the stunner in the other. Free of the chamber, he paused. To charge ahead into a blaster was stupid. Logic took over, forced control that his rage had broken. Do not run into death—hunt, trail, use what cunning he had.

He studied the dial on his palm. The needle swung to his left, in the general direction of the ruined chamber in which he had found the dead man. Here it was dark; his sight was still dazzled by the lights that had snapped into nothingness at the firing of the blaster. But the dark could be a cloak as well as a disadvantage. Also he remembered the way well enough. With his shoulder against the wall, Diskan crept along the curve.

The buzz of the device was less strong; his quarry must be well ahead. But the needle pointed fixedly on. And he would find him—most certainly he would find him!

Behind him forces he did not sense stirred.

He was close; he must not get away. So close we were, brothers!

Let him go; he is useless to us now. To himself he has returned. Perhaps he is not for our shaping.

Close! There was a chorus of that, beating down doubts.

Until he comes again to the threshold by his own wish, he is useless. Let him seek now his kind; let that be the test.

There was opposition, ready and hot, but it was overruled.

If he goes to his death, then that is the ordained pattern, and we cannot change it by all the arts. We cannot be whole with that which is flawed. He must aid in his own shaping, or the shape will be imperfect. Let him go free to do what is in him to do. Only when he has freed himself can he enter the portal we open to him. We watch, we wait, but we cannot move until he is again with an open mind and heart.

So close—Wistful, regretting.

Close, yes. But now, waiting— Our renewal is delayed; we cannot change that, for any recharging will take time, much time.

Diskan entered the room with the broken walls, his eyes turned away from the pile of stones that was now a tomb. In the dim light of the room, he could see the needle pointed to one of the wall rents. Crazy to go in there without a torch, without any hope of seeing what lay ahead, while the one he hunted could be in ambush. But, crazy or not, he was going!

An incautious step among the rubble, and he fell heavily. As he lay there for a moment, he heard a sound ahead, and the com buzzed more loudly. His teeth clenched, Diskan crawled on, taking that one small precaution against a blast.

Oddly enough, as he thrust head and shoulders through the hole, he did not come into absolute darkness such as he thought existed beyond the walls. Instead, once past that barrier, he found gray half light, and he was not far from another stair. But this curled down and not up.

Reaching that, Diskan lay flat, his ear pressed to the floor. Faint sounds—feet on the steps? The enemy was moving away. But to be trapped on the stair, a target from raying from below—

He waited until the sounds were so faint that he could hardly distinguish them. And then he swung over, planted his feet on the steps, and began to descend, but with caution.

The buzz of the device was faint, a click instead of a steady beat. When he held it to his eyes, the needle changed with every curve of the stair.

Round and around, down and down. He was already certain he must be well below the level of the streets without. There was damp rising from the stairwell, and with it an unpleasant odor of decay, such as might issue from a swamp. Perhaps there was some

103

underground outlet on the marsh bog that had come to partially swallow Xcothal.

He had to slow his descent; the rounds of the stair were making him dizzy. And once, during one of those pauses, he heard a sound from behind. Diskan pushed against the wall, his head up, peering up the corkscrew.

Outlined in the dim light was a round furred head. The animals! At least one of them was trailing him. He had used the stunner freely back there in the chamber. Had his art turned friend into enemy? But when he halted, that one halted, too, did not strive to draw closer. After a long moment, Diskan relaxed. In a way, this was a return to his first days on this world of mysteries, when he had been dogged across the ridge by just such a follower. He began to descend again.

How deep was that curl of stairway? He had not tried to count the steps, but at long last, they brought him to a firm footing from which a passage ran. And here the swamp had thrust exploring fingers.

The dank air was filled with evil odors. There were unwholesome, faintly glowing growths on the wall in leprous patches, others noduling up from the floor. Diskan had never seen a place he liked less. Yet the device told him his way lay ahead, and he could see traces of another's passing—broken fungi growths and smears on the slimy floor.

Those ragged wall growths made it difficult to see clearly. Diskan picked a very slow and cautious path, listening always—for the sound of footsteps before him, to the buzz of the com, for the animal behind. The latter he did not hear at all, but the ticking of the com approached a steady purr once more.

It was lighter down here than it had been aloft, from the luminescence of those monstrous and contorted growths. So foul was their general appearance that Diskan took every precaution to avoid any direct contact with them. But he inadvertently brushed the

104

back of his hand against a spike of fleshy stuff broken by the passing of the one he trailed.

He might have put his hand into flames, the pain bringing back a swift memory of the hurt he had taken to dis-con the watcher robot. Then the powers of the ship had healed his wound. Now he could only rub his knuckles across the skirt of the parka, hoping he was removing the irritating ooze, not smearing it in. There was an angry puffing at the base of his fingers, and he felt sharp stabs of pain when he tried to flex them.

More of the broken "branches" hung ahead, making him squirm and twist to avoid their dripping poison. Why had the enemy not used his blaster to burn clear a passage?

Diskan knew very little about those weapons. Legally, they could be worn and used only by off-worlders on planets certified dangerous, and by those of the Service. The ordinary galactic citizen had no reason to use them. He presumed they were charged much the same as the stunners, with a measure of energy that would become exhausted. And if the man ahead had not used his now to burn off this fungi for a clear passage, it could mean that his present blaster charge was low.

For the first time in hours, Diskan examined the pointer on the stunner. He had used it on the scavenger and had sprayed his path clear with it above. And it had read only half charged when he had found it. Now that small black line rested very close to the red "empty." So if the enemy lacked weapon power, he was hardly any better off. Still, he had no intention of retracing his way up into the open.

What had brought the man he tracked down into this hell hole? Flight from a stronger party? If so, where had that enemy gone? The animals? No, the dead man aloft had been blaster-killed, and up in the great hall, the blaster had been aimed at Diskan, not into the mass of furred ones among which he had knelt. So the other must have believed him part of the threat that had driven him into hiding.

Ahead was an open space cleared of all the growth, save for some shriveled, tendrils and ash on the floor. A blaster had been used here systematically, to clean a long stretch of wall on both sides of the passage. And carvings had been laid bare by that burning—not eroded into faint shadows as they had been above, but deep and clear, though discolored by the countless years the fungi had rooted over them.

Not pictures but runes, truly runes! Only the sweep of those markings held no sense as they followed curves not lines over the walls, both horizontally and vertically, in such an involved massing that it was very difficult to separate any one mark from the rest.

Four blocks, two to a wall, faced each other. And smashed before one lay a mass of glass and metal, which was surely off-world in origin. Beside it a broken coil of voice tape, snapped and snarled upon itself, coiled in a never-to-be untangled knot. Diskan's com device was purring in a rising beat. He avoided the tangle of tape and reached the part of the passage beyond where the growths began again.

"Grufa na sandank—forwarre!"

That shout could have come from anywhere ahead, but Diskan thought it sounded close, too close. And the words had no meaning. He took shelter behind a bulge of fungi. That could have been nothing but a warning. The high voice had held a note of hysteria, which was a further deterrent to plunging headlong up the passage. This place was enough to turn a man's mind. Diskan could well believe that whoever shouted might ray anything or anyone who had him cornered.

"Who are you?" Diskan tried to make that sound calm and natural. He spoke Basic and waited for an answer he hoped might make sense.

"You make no fools of us, Jack Scum. Come on and you'll be rayed!"

Basic was used for reply this time, but that did not make any more sense as far as he was concerned.

"I don't know who your Jack Scum may be," Diskan called. "I don't know who you are either. I am a wreck
106

survivor landed here by chance. My name is Diskan Fentress."

"Wearing a Jack coat?" There was scornful disbelief in that. "You have to the count of five; then we shall fire the wall growths. The smoke of their burning will stifle you!"

"Wearing a coat I found in a survivor cache," Diskan returned hurriedly. So that was why he had been rayed up there. His parka labeled him one of the enemy. "I tell you—my spacer cracked up here. I've been wandering around—"

"I don't believe you. Kal nadra sonk!"

"All right, I'm going." He stepped back into the cleared space. This business of the smoke from burning wall growths being suffocating could be true, but if his guess was right, they would not waste blaster fire.

He glanced around. Carefully, in the middle of the passage well away from the walls, stood one of the animals, its head up, watching him. It moved a step or two, limping, and Diskan knew it for the one that had shared the fight in the pass. It came on slowly to stand beside him, facing down passage. And Diskan had the feeling that again they were ranged against a common foe.

A murmur from beyond, not loud enough for him to distinguish words, just enough for him to guess that there were more than one waiting up there.

"No—you cannot! Please, High One, come back—please!"

That high voice, again strung to nervous protest. There was movement ahead. A figure lurched, apparently out of the wall, with another and slighter one dragging back at it. The larger took a step or two in Diskan's direction, then crashed on the slimed floor, pulling the other with it. Diskan sprang forward, using the stunner, knowing this was his chance.

Both of the figures lay still, caught in the bonds of the beam. A moment later he was standing over them, stooping to search for their weapons.

A Zacathan! The soft folds of the neck and head frill spread out behind the alien's head. His yellow-gray skin almost matched the color of the growths. The large reptilian eyes stared up at Diskan, though there was an oddly unfocused quality in them. Above the alien's waist the tight fabric of a protecto-suit had been cut away to allow bandaging of his torso; then plasta-skin had been poured over the wide folds.

His smaller companion also stared at Diskan as he rolled the body over, but those eyes were very aware, filled with fear and loathing. A girl, her hair tumbling out of a net, her protecto-suit smeared and scraped—and in her belt what he was seeking, the blaster. He transferred that before he looked around.

There was a gap in the wall, a rough-hewn doorway. They must have come through there. He moved to explore the space beyond. He found two supply bags, a bedroll spread out, an ever-burn lamp, and a jumble of other things piled against the far wall—but no one else.

Diskan lifted the girl and carried her in, to drop her on the bedroll. Then he made the same trip with the Zacathan, whom he stretched out on the floor. The alien's skin was harsh and dry to the touch; he was manifestly fevered, perhaps seriously hurt.

With his hands on his hips, Diskan looked from one to the other. Survivors from a crashed ship would not be wearing protecto-suits. Those were the issue of some government service to be used by planet explorers. He did not know how long he would have to wait before they came out from under the effects of the stunner beam and he would be able to ask some questions, but now he had plenty of time.

ELEVEN

The furred one stretched out across the doorway, now and again gazing out into the passage, listening perhaps, Diskan thought. He himself prowled the room, inspecting the material piled there. Then he triggered a tape reader, which had a spool set in it.

"Report 6A3, Mimir Expedition. Fifth day since we holed up. Hist Techneer Zimgrald suffering from his wound, has been alternating between unconsciousness and fevered raving. Necessary for me to go above to see whether we are still being hunted. Will record again upon my return. Julha Than signing off."

"Julha Than," Diskan repeated, peering down at the girl, who watched him with those hating eyes. "I am Diskan Fentress—" Could he be sure—? He thought that there had been a change in her icy regard when he repeated his name. On impulse, he struggled out of the tight parka so she could see his Vaan tunic, spotted and worn as it was.

"It was the truth I told you," he added. "I survived a spacer crash; my ship was swallowed up in a mud bog. And I found a cache—that's where I got this coat."

As long as the stunner held, she could not answer, but she would have to listen, not being able to thrust her fingers into her ears as he had in the Vaanchard garden.

"I don't know what has been going on here. I found a dead man under some rubble in the room this passage stair heads from. He was wearing this, and that is what led me to you—after you tried to ray me." Diskan held the device in her line of vision. "Believe me, I'm not after you. I have no reason to fight—"

He thought that he had at that moment when he had stormed out of the chamber after the fleeing sniper. However, that rage had cooled. Now he could understand the mistake about the parka. He turned away from the girl and went to kneel beside the Zacathan. There was nothing he could do for the alien. His medical knowledge was nil; he had had no intensive briefing in first aid such as all members of an expedition were given. Doubtless the girl had already done all she could for the alien.

Diskan was impatient for the stun effect to wear off, to ask questions. Once more he turned to the tape reader. There were other disks fitted in below the speaker. Diskan awkwardly freed the tape in the flow bars and took the first one from the small rack to snap in its place.

"Report 2B1." He thought he recognized the girl's clipped speech. "The firing of the wall growth produces a nauseous and perhaps dangerous effect. We have withdrawn to the side chamber, leaving the port-blast on remote control. There is good evidence that the deductions are correct, that the 'Place of Great Riches' lies near here and we may well uncover the clue in this wall search. Captain Ranbo and his two crewmen have gone for more heat-unit charges and to secure the ship during our work here. Julha Than, Second Tech, reporting."

Click, click, click, and then the voice began again:

"Report 2B2. Heat unit in the port-blast exhausted, but use was successful. Wall shows excellent series of carvings—see vid tape 884. First Tech Mik s'Fan has gone to explore ahead. Have received two progress signals from him. Captain Ranbo and his men have not returned yet. We cannot use the in-probe without the stepped-up beamer they are to bring. Using this
110

period to make detailed scan-vid record of uncovered walls."

Again the clicking interval. Then another voice, harsher, with a hissing intonation—without doubt, that of the Zacathan. And this dictated portion was couched in a technical code that meant nothing to Diskan. That flowed on and on until the tape was exhausted. Diskan put the rewound disk back in its slot and selected one from farther along.

"Report 5D5. No reply from First Tech s'Fan in eight planet hours. Have set recall three hours ago, putting it on urgent. Have tried to reach Captain Ranbo also. No reply since the garbled message of an hour ago. The animals are on the stairway and seem hostile, keeping us from ascending. Hist Tech Zimgrald does not want to incite them, for the reasons he stated in his earlier report. Since they test, even by our crude methods, about 8 over X or more, he is striving to establish contact by the Four Rules. They do not move against us, but neither will they permit us to leave here. Have set both ship call and summoner on full and locked them."

There was an interval and then Julha's voice, not precise or controlled this time, but high in tone, her words coming fast and slurred:

"Report 5D6. Message from ship, cut off after a few words. Ship under attack; no answer from s'Fan. The animals are still guarding the stair, making no move at us—"

The message broke off, and there was nothing more on the tape. Diskan pulled out the next and threaded it in.

"Report 5—5D—" Plainly, Julha had been uncertain of the proper numeration. Her voice was strained, and she spoke haltingly.

"After the animals disappeared, we went up the stair. No sign of anything amiss above. The trail markers were still up, but we tried twice to get out of the city and found ourselves lost. Have no explanation for this. At nightfall, returned to the tower-temple.

111

Animals gathered in the usual way in the great hall. Tried to enter, but two barred the way. We have returned to base camp here. No messages recorded while we were gone. I asked the High One to put me under hypo-sleep again tonight—the dreams have been growing worse. He wishes me to allow them and record by brain-read, but they frighten me so I cannot stand that. No animals on the stair. We shall prepare emergency packs and try again tomorrow to leave the city. Cannot see how the markers became so confused. Hist Tech Zimgrald will now add to this report—"

The Zacathan in his own code completed the tape. Diskan looked once again at the girl.

"So you couldn't get out of the city either," he commented. "What happens to those streets when one tries to make the ridge? Does it affect everyone? And you had markers to follow—"

Her eyes were no longer wary or fearful. She was surveying him now as if he were a problem that interested rather than repelled her.

"Now"—Diskan reached for the neighboring disk—"what happened next?"

"Report 6A1. Set out at dawn for a new try to return to the ship. Saw party of three coming in—watched them from town lookout. The High One believes them to be Jacks. Remained on the upper walk. As they drew near, we noted animals about them, but in hiding. We kept to cover, but thought it best to withdraw to lower levels. Can only be old story of the treasure drawing them for a grab. If so, we may be alone, and Captain Ranbo and his men are—are already dead." There was a pause before she continued to record. "Hist Tech Zimgrald wishes to record that he believes this to be a Defense One action. He is unsealing arms, and we shall each carry them. The call for Mik s'Fan has dead-offed, and we have no unit to step it up. As far as we know, we are now alone—"

"We were—"

Diskan jerked around. She had moved on the bedroll and levered herself up with the use of her arms,

112

manifestly fighting the muscle weakness left by the ray. "Please, help me up. Get the High One on the bed here. The bleeding must not begin again—I have no more plasta-skin or curb shots!"

He aided her to sit with her back supported against the wall and then hoisted the Zacathan carefully to the improvised bed.

"The Jacks shot him?"

"In a way. They had begun to burn holes in the walls up there. They plainly knew something of what they were hunting for—some of the ship's people must have been made to talk. The High One was trying to watch them, and there was a break—he was caught under a wall fall. I think they believed him dead, and that was when I saw their captain, wearing that—" She pointed to Diskan's discarded parka. "Why they didn't come on down here, I can't tell. But they hurried away. I got the High One from under the stone; he didn't seem so badly hurt then. Somehow we came down the stair here, but later he collapsed, and ever since—" She spread out her hands in a gesture of helplessness.

"And the dead man up there?"

She shivered, covered her face. "Later, I went up— He came after me, and I fired— I never really knew what happened."

"But they did not come down here?"

"No. I—I thought you were one of them. The animals —they come and look at us, then go. I thought you were going to use them against us. I've—" Julha gave a shaky laugh. "I've tried to talk to them, but it's no good. They are intelligent, you know; the High One is sure of that. But we haven't been able to establish any method of communication."

"You say these Jacks knew what they were after. Just what is that?"

Julha did not answer immediately but caught her lip between her teeth, as if to muffle any speech while she thought it over. Then she must have made her decision in favor of trusting him, for she began to talk swiftly.

113

"This planet was recorded about twenty years ago by a First-in Scout—Renfry Fentress." She stared at Diskan round-eyed. "Fentress—you?"

Diskan shook his head. "My father."

"Yes, I did not think you could be that old, unless you were mutant. Well, he vid-pictured the ruins as part of his report. And the Zacathan archivists became interested. They have the legend repository for this section of the galaxy, and every once in a while they think—and usually they are right—that they can uncover pieces of the Forerunners' history by exploring the base of such legends. This was one of those times.

"And, as most always, the rumor got out it was a treasure hunt, especially since the High One Zimgrald was put in charge of the expedition. He's made two very rich and exciting finds in the past—the Shining Palace of Slang and the Voorjan grave sites. Both of those were fabulously rich, though their archaeological value was beyond price. These legend hunts are always a gamble—

"Anyway, the Zacathans got exploratory rights here, with all claims to archaeological finds. They assembled a mixed staff according to regulations. I'm a Second Archaeological Techneer from New Britain, Mik was from Larog, and Captain Ranbo and his men, our two lab techneers, were all on loan from Survey."

"A small expedition," Diskan commented.

"Yes, but we were just to do the prelim survey, and then the real field force would come in, if and when our reports made it worthwhile."

"And you thought it would be worthwhile?"

"The High One did. We don't understand the whole process of legend tracing. The Zacathans are so much longer lived than we, and they have techniques of learning and mental storage we cannot equal. I know there is something here that excited the High One greatly. And I am sure we were traced by these Jacks because they are determined to loot what we do find. They can sell such treasure in any of a hundred or so undercover trading centers!"

114

"But—where did they go?" Diskan sat back on his heels. "I found a place where a ship or ships had planeted, and near there was a survivor cache—with its broadcaster on."

"But didn't that broadcast tell you who they were?"

Diskan shook his head. "Not in Basic."

"Then our people didn't leave it for us!" She folded her hands together. "I thought—perhaps they had to take off and had left it. Only they would have set a standard signal call."

"No. I got this coat there. And there were a lot of sealed containers, personal locked. Must have been a dump for one special crowd."

"Then, wherever they went, they intend to come back. But where did they go? And our ship—it must have gone also. Why?"

Diskan considered those questions. Suddenly, he knew that for the first time in his life, he was thinking swiftly and clearly, able to translate thought into speech unhaltingly. And he had a lift of new self-confidence.

"You said another ship was going to follow you here. Would they be waiting for some signal?"

"Yes—oh, yes. They were to conclude the work on Zoraster. And if our report was negative, they would then return to home base."

Diskan nodded. "There you have one possible explanation. Your ship could be used to deliver such a report. They might have this Captain Ranbo or some other member of his crew under hypo-control. Your second ship gets the negative and takes off for home base, leaving the Jacks free from interference, with plenty of time to clean up here."

"And they could be coming again—now!"

Diskan had picked up the com device from where he had laid it beside the tape reader. "What's this? And how does it work to track someone?"

"We use those to check on our people while exploring. There's always a chance of an accident, a need for rescue. When we're in the field, one of those can be

115

tuned to an individual." She took the dial from him, examined it closely, and then looked up, a shadow of fear in her eyes.

"This has been select-set for me!"

"And they must have found it on your ship?"

She nodded.

"And so they could have one set for him, too?" Diskan indicated the Zacathan.

"I'm not sure, not without a lot of adjustment, which they may not know how to do. It works differently with Zacathans because they are telepathic."

"But if they do have one, they'll head straight here."

"Yes, but we can't get him up those stairs!"

"No, only there is the passage running on from this room."

"Mik went that way—" Julha's voice was very low.

"We may have a lot of time," Diskan told her, "we may have very little. But staying here, we have no chance at all. Have you any high Sustain? Enough to get him on his feet?"

"But moving him that way—it could kill him!"

"And staying here might kill him, and us, too. Or—knowing who he is, they might not want to kill him. He'd be a tool for them—after they broke him properly." Diskan was brutally frank, and he saw her flinch from the thoughts his words brought to mind.

"The young man is entirely right—" Delivered in a slow hiss, that statement drew their eyes to the Zacathan.

Though he still lay stretched on the pallet where Diskan had placed him, his eyes were now focused on his companions with the light of full understanding in them.

"High One!" Julha came away from the wall. He raised one four-digit, talon-clawed hand.

"He is right," Zimgrald repeated slowly. "These scavengers would like nothing better than to have such a key as me to turn in many locks. Thus, they must not have it—ever. Were it not that I can be, I believe, of some small service to our general purpose still, I would

116

make sure of that myself. I do not think that I am unduly concerned with my own future when I say this to you. There is that here which perhaps can be swayed to your aid—if I can remain with you to aid— Your true help lies there—"

With infinite labor, he turned his hand to point to the furred one, still lying across the threshold.

"There is a way through these ruins that those know and use. Learn it from then, and you can hide indefinitely from any hunters. Haaa—"

The call he uttered was low, hissing, and directed to the furred one. The animal's head swung around, and it favored the Zacathan with one of those unwinking stares by which it, or its kind, had disconcerted Diskan in the past. Now the creature got to its feet and limped over to the Zacathan. Reptilian man and furred one matched stares for long enough to make Diskan uneasy.

"I cannot touch thoughts with it directly," Zimgrald reported at long last, "but it is my hope that it now understands that we are in peril here and must go hence. Whether it will be our guide, I have no assurance.

"Even with Sustain, High One, you cannot climb the stair," Julha protested.

"That is also right. Therefore, we must take the other road—along the passage."

"Mik—" Her lips shaped the name rather than uttered it aloud.

"Mik, yes, he went that way and he did not return. But for all of us, there is little other choice. To climb those stairs might be walking straight into the arms of the enemy. Whereas"—his yellow lips curved in a half smile—"we may leave behind us here that which will discourage followers—even if only temporarily. There are tools that can be weapons at need. Now, do you do thus—"

From the pallet, he gave quick yet clear directions. Things were sorted out of the general mass of the piled supplies and combined to his liking, though

117

Diskan found that a measure of his old fumbling awkwardness returned. When the girl grew impatient at his ineptitude, the Zacathan sent her to make packs of the supplies they must carry. Under the alien's patient and concise exposition, Diskan became more sure.

In the end, he had a framework of tubing, to which had been attached by wire the high-voltage ever-burn lamp. He did not understand just what the contraption would do, but the Zacathan's reliance on the queer assembly was high, and Diskan was sure that Zimgrald was certain of its efficiency.

This was placed across the passage, a frail enough barrier. The furred one watched Diskan's actions with concentrated interest. When the young man returned to the room, Julha was on her knees by the pallet, about to administer a Sustain injection to the Zacathan.

"It would be good to know," Zimgrald remarked, "how much time the Armored Spirit allows us before disaster swoops like a grahawk. But that is another of the puzzles past our solving. Do not hesitate, little one. I am as eager to be away from this hole as the twain of you!"

His reaction to the reviving injection came swiftly, and when he got to his feet, he moved with only a small hesitation. Diskan swung the larger pack to his back; the girl took up the smaller. They went into the passage where the furred one lingered. As they came out, the animal turned and limped along the unknown way, Zimgrald at its heels with Julha, while Diskan brought up the rear. He glanced back once at the framework of the device he had set up in the corridor. According to the Zacathan, it would deter pursuit; Diskan had no idea how. He only trusted that it would.

TWELVE

Zimgrald carried a torch but did not snap it on. The diffusion of light from the growths appeared to satisfy the Zacathan. Diskan could see no other sign that anyone else had trod this way before them. He began to marvel at the recuperative powers of the Hist Techneer, for Zimgrald was keeping a gliding pace equaling a fast walk for his two companions, while a little to the fore limped the furred one as guide.

"High One." Julha touched the shoulder of the Zacathan. "That Sustain shot, it will wear off—"

"All the greater reason, little one, for us to make speed now." There was an almost cheerful note in the alien's voice. "Do not concern yourself; our bodies are not alike. I shall perhaps surprise you with my ability to keep the trail. Fentress—" He raised his voice a little so the name boomed back at Diskan.

"Yes?"

"What is your knowledge of this world?"

"Very little. My ship crashed at setdown and rolled into one of the mud pools. I had been in freeze and so was lucky, for the emergency ejector got me out. There was a rising ridge of solid ground, and I came along that. Then I found the survivor cache—"

"And the city. But not without guidance. Now that is the truth, is it not? Guidance such as this." One of the four-digited yellow-gray hands gestured toward the furred one.

"Yes—"

"But you are the son of the Scout who first discovered Mimir. You must know more—" There was pressure behind that, Diskan knew. Perhaps the Zacathan had his own suspicions under his outward acceptance of Diskan.

But Diskan was not going to spill all his own past history at the bidding of this alien, even if that would settle the other's doubts.

"A First-in Scout visits many planets during his service. Not even he can remember them without a tape—" The minute he said that, Diskan knew he had made a mistake.

"A tape—ah, yes. You crashed on Mimir. Yet this world is far from any transport lane, Fentress. It is not on any commercial or open-travel voyage tape. There would be no normal reason for you to visit Mimir."

"I came for reasons of my own!" Diskan snapped.

He could see the pale oval of Julha's face as she glanced back, though Zimgrald had not turned his head. And Diskan thought that, even in this dim light, he could see the wariness again in her eyes.

"Reasons that might have something to do with those who seek us?" The Zacathan continued to probe.

"No!" Diskan hoped that the very explosiveness of that reply would carry the accent of truth. "Until my ship planeted here, I did not even know Mimir existed."

"Yet your ship came on tape if you were in freeze." No hint of suspicion, yet Diskan knew that he must satisfy the other or those questions would chip away at him.

"Yes, my ship was on tape, but I did not know the tape destination. It was blind chance that it was Mimir. I'm not a pilot; the ship was on auto. I don't even know why it crashed. I wasn't curious until it started the ride down and failed. Why the ship was on tape is my business, but I'll swear by any power you want to name that it had nothing to do with what you have met here!"

120

To his own ears that sounded a little too quick, too emphatic. Under the circumstances, he was not sure that had he been Zimgrald, he would have believed it. He was sure that Julha did not, for she walked faster, close to the Zacathan, lengthening the space between them. And perversely, Diskan allowed her to do that. Let them believe it or not—he had told the truth.

"You have satisfied my curiosity acceptably, Fentress. These oddities of blind chance do exist, as no one can deny. The X factor—"

"X factor?" Diskan repeated. Had the Zacathan meant what he said? Did he believe that Diskan was speaking the truth or was he only willing, for now, to accept the explanation, cloaking his doubts?

"Yes, the X factor—that which comes of itself to throw askew equations, speculations, lives, history, that unknown twist or turn of small events that changes a man's personal future, the work he would do, or the future of a people and an empire from one possibility track to another. One may have a problem close to smooth solving. Then the X factor arises to make the simple complex, all calculations wrong. Thus, to Mimir you may be the X factor, and to you Mimir may be the same. So I believe.

"This chance we cannot control or understand may have delivered you here at just this time. Ah—" There came a sound not unlike a human chuckle. "How interesting life may become without warning! This Mimir is a world of many puzzles; perhaps we shall add to that number. Now—what have we here?"

The passage ended. Julha gave a little cry, which held an undercurrent of fear. Diskan moved up to join them.

There was a vast expanse broken only by lines of huge blocks supporting a ceiling above, rising out of a weird marsh.

Though Zimgrald switched on the lamp, sending its powerful beam down the aisles between the pillars, it revealed nothing but pools of murky water, the fungi growths, a nightmare of swamp. The furred one lowered

121

its head to sniff at the edge of a pool reaching to their feet. It hissed, spat, made a lightning-swift dab with a forepaw. There were ripples on the surface of the water, sending bobbing several padlike plants floating there. Then the Mimiran animal sat up on its haunches to look at the off-worlders. In warning? Diskan wondered.

Dare he try contact? He knew the danger of that reaching out, or thought he did. Why did it come to mind again now and with so strong an urge? He pushed aside fear and tried to reach the brain behind those burning eyes.

There was a sensation of dizzy spinning, of being caught and whirled about by a power much stronger than he was. Diskan heard himself cry out. He was in a panic because no effort of his could free him from the spin.

"Diskan!"

His head bobbed loosely on his shoulders; he swayed in the grip of the Zacathan on the very edge of that poisonous pool. Still the furred one sat upright, watching, reaching. Reaching, that was it! Of his own free will, Diskan had opened a door and through it something had reached for him, almost sucked him out into an unknown so appalling that he shuddered with the sickness the thought of it aroused in him. Had he been lost in that unthinkable, he would never have returned.

With the Zacathan's hands still on him, Diskan backed away from the animal, feeling as weak as if he had survived, just barely survived, some indescribable ordeal.

"What happened?" Zimgrald's voice in Diskan's ear was very steadying, as if he leaned his whole trembling body against a solid and sustaining support.

"I—I tried to make mental contact with—with that!"

His hand rose almost of itself and pointed stiffly at the furred one. The outthrust fingers might have been a stunner he was aiming in his own defense.

"Contact? You are a xeno-path?"

122

"I—sometimes I can make an animal, or a bird, do as I wish. Before I was afraid, but I did it now, I don't know why—!"

"And you found far more than you expected." No question, a brisk statement of fact. "Yes, these are telepaths to a high degree, though not of any order I have had previous knowledge of. But, again, this is luck. If you can establish better communication with them than I have been able to do—"

Diskan twisted free from the other's hold. "No! Never again! I tell you, it—it would take me!" He tried to explain, and his old inability to fit words and thoughts neatly together made him stammer. He was ready to defend himself from such a risk with a stunner—with his bare hands if need be!

Then common sense reasserted control. The Zacathan could not *make* him try contact, not unless the alien put him under some form of hypo-control. And he would make sure that did not happen. Diskan was about to voice that defiance when they were startled by a sound echoing down the passage from which they had just emerged.

Zimgrald's features, with their lizard cast, sharpened; his neck frill arose in a wide fan behind head and shoulders.

"So, they found our surprise." His words were close to a hiss. "We have very little time after all!"

Julha caught at the Zacathan's arm. "High One, what do we do?"

The Zacathan's frill fluttered and began to refold. "Why, little one, we splash forward—or rather we pick the best footing possible." He looked at the furred one. "This one knows what we want—escape. It will, I believe, continue to aid us. Certain emotions are strong enough to project in themselves—fear, hate, love—and fear we shall depend upon now to do our pleading for us. But it is best we move on. That surprise will deter them from the trail for a space, but it is no lasting barrier."

But they did not go forward, out into the swamp.

123

The furred one dropped to all fours and headed right, along the wall through which the passage had entered. Zimgrald appeared quite content to follow the animal's lead. A hand on Diskan's arm, he pulled the young man forward, Julha on his other side.

Once again the Zacathan switched off the lamp. Diskan was about to protest when he saw the wisdom of that action. The far-flung beam might not only advertise their coming to some unknown menace ahead, but it could also be sighted readily by those following.

Here the luminescence of the growths was not quite so concentrated as it had been in the passage, but there was enough radiance to show them their footing, and the animal's, a few paces in advance.

"What is this place?" Julha ventured after they had gone a short way.

"Who knows?" Zimgrald answered. "For some reason, the city builders needed it. These piers must support a goodly portion of buildings above. But the why of this cave? Who can tell that?" His frill lifted a little as he shrugged. "In its time it had a use or it would not be. This city has always been wedded to water—"

"Yes," Diskan broke in dreamily, "the flowing streets, the cool, clean flowing streets—"

"Yes," prompted the Zacathan gently. "What of these flowing streets?"

For a second of time Diskan was back in his dream. "Sweet water, scented water—water of the streets of Xcothal—" His voice trailed off as he came out of that half spell and knew that both of them were listening to him alertly.

"You have dreamed?" Not gently now—a demand, quick and pressing.

"Once I walked in Xcothal with the water washing about me." Diskan gave the alien the truth.

"And what did you learn of Xcothal when you walked thus?"

"That it was beauty, color, light—a very fair place."

"And that you would walk there again if you could?"
124

"Yes—" At that admission he felt the Zacathan's grasp on his arm tighten and then relax.

"So they reached you—with that they reached you! You see, little one." Zimgrald spoke to the girl. "The dreams are not evil; they were reaching—"

She shook her head emphatically. "No! Those dreams were horrible; they threatened! I did not walk streets of water in beauty; I fled through dark hallways and ever they hunted me!"

"Who?" Diskan asked. "The Jacks?"

Again she shook her head, with even more force. "No, I never saw who—only knew that they wanted me. And it was very bad. We did not dream alike, though I, too, was in a city—"

"Xcothal—" Zimgrald repeated the name thoughtfully. "This name for the city, it is from your dream?"

"It is. And this is Xcothal—but not the one I saw then."

"Living flesh for a moment laid across the crumbling bones. You have some strange gift, Fentress, one that I envy you. In my mind I can build a picture when I look out over tumbled stones and long deserted buildings. Training, memory, surmise all give me bits to fit together into a picture, but I know that never is the picture the full truth. Sometimes it may fit close, but a line is wrong here and a curve there—"

Diskan had an inspiration. "The X factor?"

Zimgrald chuckled again. "Undoubtedly—the X factor. It is missing for me; it may not be for you. Perhaps you can evoke the picture that fits perfectly!"

"I'm no archaeologist."

"What are you, Diskan Fentress?" asked the Zacathan.

The old bitterness shadowed his reply. "Nothing—nothing at all. No—" The desire arose in him to shock, to break the Zacathan's calm. "That is not the truth. I am a criminal—a subject for stabilizing treatment if I am found!"

Julha missed a step, but Zimgrald gave a small sound like a snort.

"I do not doubt that either, Fentress; you are so proud of it, as a definite victory for you. But why do you consider it a victory? What life-vise are you fleeing in such haste? No, do not fret—I shall not pick below the surface you have chosen to shell you in. Only you are far more than you guess. Do not crawl into the mud when you can soar. Ha—do you notice anything about the atmosphere now, children?"

The quick change of subject left Diskan tongue-tied, but Julha responded.

"It is warmer!"

"I thought so, though the Sustain has given me protection against any chill. Now why is this so?"

Not only was it indeed warmer—the warmest Diskan had known, save directly by the fireside, since he had landed on Mimir—but the rank air carried another taint. Zimgrald sniffed, drawing in deep breaths and expelling them several times, before he gave a small nod.

"Warm springs, perhaps. A natural phenomenon, but hardly to be expected under a city, though we should always disabuse our minds of the 'expected.' There is never just *what* we expect. Our friend waits—"

The Mimiran animal had indeed halted at the foot of a broad stone, slimed here and there with splotches of evil-looking growths, angled to their left and lifting at an incline out into the open marsh. Zimgrald surveyed what they could see of it.

"A bridge of sorts. But watch the footing. On stone, those slime patches can be highly treacherous."

"They were!" Julha darted forward, to pick up and bring back a gleaming object. She held it out to Zacathan. "Mik dropped this!"

"A refill tube for a hand beam." Zimgrald identified it. "Yes, we might reasonably suppose this to be s'Fan's." He clicked on his more powerful lamp, bringing into brilliant focus that rising arch of stone and its approaches. Well up the incline was a smear. A body crushing one of the growths in a fall could well have left that sign.

126

"Mik!" Julha clapped her hands together. "He must be ahead of us—on this very way! He could still be alive, he could be!"

"It is possible," Zimgrald agreed. But inwardly Diskan doubted that the Zacathan was any more hopeful of finding the missing explorer than he was. "No, child." The alien put out a hand to restrain Julha. "Hurry here we do not! We cannot risk any accidents. See, observe the caution of our guide—"

The furred one had started up the bridge, if bridge it was, but as the Zacathan pointed out, the animal advanced with caution, weaving a crooked way that took it around those slime patches. And, gingerly, the three fell into a single line, to track in the same way.

As they went, the chemical fumes grew thicker, rising from the swamp. The reek reached them in puffs, as if exhaled in regular gasps. Once up the first approach, the ramp ceased to climb but leveled off and ran, as a rampart or road, straight out between two ranks of the thick block supports, into the general gloom of the cavern.

For spaces, the slime patches failed and the furred one hurried. Then would come another line of splotches, and they went back to their weaving in and out among them. Diskan thought that their guide not only feared the slipperiness of those smears but also knew that contact with them was dangerous. He remembered the stinging burn from the growth he had brushed against back in the passage and decided that such caution was well merited.

"Where can the end of this be?" Julha asked at last.

Time was only relative to action, Diskan knew, but they *had* been walking this raised road for what seemed a long period. He glanced back several times, trying to make out the wall from which they had come, but the limited light from the fungi made shadows close in behind them, and he could see very little. Meanwhile, the ramp stretched endless before them.

"The end, little one, is when and where we find it." Zimgrald answered her with a tired slur to his words.

She must have noted that at once, for she caught at the Zacathan's hand, held it in both of hers.

"High One, you tire! We must rest, eat, see to you!"

Diskan half expected the Zacathan to deny that, and he was disturbed when the alien nodded agreement. Was the other beginning to fail?

"As always, little one, you speak with good sense. Yes, let us rest, for a short space only. And eat. Those are good thoughts to put into action."

They sat down in one of the spaces free from the slime, and the girl opened her pack, taking out ration tubes of a like brand to those Diskan had found in the cache. But she made the Zacathan swallow a tablet before he sucked at what was a mixture of food and drink in the container.

Diskan hesitated and then twisted in half the tube he held, the material of it coming apart under his strength, hardened by those years of physical labor. Keeping the oozing top section, he held out the other to the furred one.

The animal arose and limped to his side. Erect on its haunches, it held the tube to its mouth and squeezed out the contents with the claws of its forepaws. Now Diskan saw why something about those claws had puzzled him at the time he had first sighted one of this species. Claws and paws, yes, but the dexterity was that of a hand, not human perhaps, but still a hand.

He glanced around to find Zimgrald watching him. "They are not animals." The Zacathan might have been speaking Diskan's own thoughts aloud. "What are they? That is a very important question—*what* are they?"

And another important question, Diskan wanted to add but did not, is what do they want with us?

128

THIRTEEN

The warmth of the underground world was lulling. Perhaps the exhalation of the swamp carried a drugging quality. Diskan had no desire to go on. Neither did either of his companions appear eager to take to their feet again. Julha was watching the Zacathan carefully.

"High One"—she broke the silence first—"is it well with you?"

The edge of his neck frill stirred. "Do not fret, little one. This old creeper will be able to creep yet farther, if for no other reason than curiosity, which will not let me rest until I see what lies at the end of the trail. It is in my mind that this was once a place of water. They loved water—those who have gone, long gone, before us. But why it must wash the deep foundations of their walls and towers, that is only to be guessed at—"

"An amphibian, water-born race?" Diskan hazarded.

"Perhaps. There are such—or were such—just as there are races who fly or creep. Yet our friend here"—he nodded to the Mimiran animal—"is not of the water."

Greatly daring, Diskan risked a question of his own. "What do the legends say of Xcothal?"

Zimgrald smiled. "Very little. A hint—such an old hint—of treasure to be found in a city of the sea—"

"Treasure!"

The Zacathan's frill was rising to frame his lizard, shadowed face. "Ah, that is a word that makes the blood run faster, does it not? But I believe that Xcothal's treasure is not that which one can hold in his two hands, count into boxes, feast the eyes upon. Oh, all races have their wealth, sometimes gathered into piles and stores. But if there was wealth such as that here once, I believe the years have seen to its scattering, and those Jacks will not find what they seek, not even if they dismantle Xcothal stone by stone—the which they are certainly not prepared to do."

"Treasure—knowledge?" Diskan speculated.

"Just so—knowledge. Always remember this, youth. Beneath the wildest tale from a people's past lies a crumb of truth. Sometimes that crumb may be very small and much distorted by rumor and legend, but it is there. And if it can be sifted free from all the accumulation of the years, then it is worth more than all the precious metal and gems a man may heap up to feast his eyes upon, for the feasting of the mind is the richer experience and lasts the longer. The hunters behind us pursue their 'treasure,' which may long since have ceased to be, but I do not believe it is the same I seek here."

"But royal tombs, storehouses—"

Zimgrald nodded. "Those can be found—and looted. And I may be wrong also. I have never claimed infallibility, my children. Look, our guide is growing impatient. I would say it is time we were once more on the tramp."

Diskan aided the Zacathan to his feet. For all his brave words to Julha earlier, it was plain that Zimgrald was failing. Their rest and food might have given the alien a return of strength, but how much longer he could keep going was a question. And as far as Diskan could see, there was no end to their present road.

The Mimiran animal, having seen them rise, turned and moved on, its head carried well up, as if it sought some airborne scent. But the odors from the waste below, Diskan thought, were enough to make anyone breathe less heavily. He kept a back watch for the enemy, but if the Jacks had passed the booby trap, they seemed in no hurry to catch up with the fugitives. Only the thought of the hunt made Diskan speed his pace until he was treading close on the heels of the other two.

"There is no need for pushing. The High One can go no faster," Julha snapped.

"I am afraid reason supports the thought that there is," Zimgrald told her. "We would present excellent targets for an attack, and I do not wish to leave this roadway unless there is no other choice."

With that, Diskan was in hearty agreement. He had the stunner with a close-to-exhausted charge and the blaster he had taken from Julha. But to stand up against a determined Jack rush with no more defense than that was sheer suicide.

A man did not turn Jack, preying on traders and colonists on frontier worlds, unless he was already an outlaw to the point of no return. And to get what they wanted, these looters would have no scruples at all. They might keep the Zacathan alive—until they had what they wanted from him. And Julha, as a woman, would be an extra bonus. Him they would burn down without a thought, and he would be the lucky one. But how could the Jacks be so sure as to center a major grab operation on Mimir? Was it just Zimgrald's reputation that had brought the pirates here—the fact that the Hist Techneer had made two outstanding archaeological finds in the past? That was a gamble nearly to the point of being stupid—and stupid the Jacks were not. Those who were died early and were not equipped for a planned raid the way these were. All they had done here bore the marks of a carefully thought out operation.

On the other hand, the Zacathan had been telling the truth a few minutes ago when he had said that the treasure he was after was not material. So, what did that mean? What secret from the past was so rich a find as to bring on a grab?

"What *do* they want here?" Diskan demanded out of his thoughts.

"Loot!" Julha said scornfully.

"But our young friend means what kind," Zimgrald said. "Yes, that has been a small puzzle among the larger for me also. They are very well prepared, these Jacks, and they have had detailed briefing on our plans. They are very sure that they are in quest of something worth such a major effort, as if they have had success promised to them. Yet I do *not* know what could be worth the risk and expenditure of this grab."

"You?" Diskan asked. Could it be that—a highly successful Hist Techneer to be kidnapped and kept on ice? But that would be pure speculation of the kind that was too great a gamble for Jacks with their need for a quick profit and an even more speedy getaway.

"Flattering." A chuckle warmed Zimgrald's voice. "But, except for how I may aid them here, I think not. The law of averages would dictate that no man can continue to make big finds year after year. No, what they seek is here, unfortunately for us. They believe that we have the secret, and that makes us important. Otherwise, they would write us off and go treasure hunting—to leave us wandering about this pile, marooned and helpless."

"Rrrrrrrugggg!"

Julha cried out. The Zacathan's frill shot up and fanned. Diskan's hand went to the butt of the blaster. The furred one, who had been silent during their whole journey through this stinking pit, had uttered that nerve-rasping cry. It stopped short and reared on its haunches, its clawed forefeet advancing a little, its muzzle gaping to show fangs. There was no mistaking that stance—it was facing danger.

Diskan shouldered past the Zacathan and Julha, shucking his pack as he went.

"Get down!" he ordered with a thought of blaster fire sweeping the ramp road. He was in a half crouch, trying to pierce the gloom ahead, to distinguish the menace there.

After that first battle cry, the Mimiran animal was silent, but Diskan could hear the faint hissing of its breath.

"Zimgrald," he cried, "use the lamp!"

The broad beam might betray them, but it would also reveal what lurked there. That was better than supine waiting for danger to come to them, perhaps in a fashion for which there was no defense.

Yellow-white was the glare behind him, making his shadow and that of the furred one great black fingers across the stone. And it also showed, only too clearly to off-world eyes, that which squatted in the middle of their path. Diskan shrank back a step before he steadied. That thing was far worse than the monster he had faced in the pass. With all its alienness, that had been akin to beasts he had known on other planets.

But this repulsive thing was akin to nothing outside of an insane nightmare. The front portion had reared up above the main bulk and was weaving to and fro, an obscene pillar, tapering, having no features Diskan could discern, save a puckered opening, which moved with the swaying, opening and closing.

Glistening trails of slime oozed down the gray hide and puddled about the fat center portion of the thing. This or its kind must have left the tracks he had found in the outer city.

Diskan's revulsion was tinged with fear. The thing was huge, twice, maybe three times, his own not inconsiderable bulk. And for all its lack of visible eyes or other sense organs, he believed it was not only aware of them but also able to spot them exactly. Every indication was that it greeted them with hostile intentions.

He brought up the blaster, leveled it at that swaying head, and then judiciously moved the sights down to the fat roundness of the mid-body. After all, there was a good chance that the thing could be better hit in that more stationary part.

"Wait!" Zimgrald's order came just as Diskan was

about to press the firing button, and such was the authority in it that Diskan obeyed.

The furred one had made one of its quick darts—not ahead at the slug thing but sidewise, against Diskan, carrying him to the right. Now the opening in the weaving pillar puckered into an outward pout and from that spouted a dark stream of liquid—too short, for it splashed against the stone merciful inches away.

Diskan fired, but his aim was poor, and the ray only clipped the pointed "head" of the creature. It writhed, looping the upheld pillar of its body in a fantastic whip of coiling and uncoiling skin and muscle. Sometimes it twisted back on its bulk in a way to suggest than any bony framework existing under those unwholesome rolls of flesh was not rigid.

"Wait!" For the second time Zimgrald rapped out that order.

But this time, Diskan was in no mind to obey. He strove to center the blaster on the middle of the bulk, only the movements of the creature were more frenzied, convulsive in their rapidity and force. Had that slight burn really done all the harm the thing's writhing now suggested?

There was a sound, as if someone had torn a length of fabric. Across the middle of the frantically threshing bulk, skin and flesh parted in a break that grew wider and wider as the motions of the creature sloughed it apart. The pillar gave a last titanic upthrust and then fell forward limply, to lie full length on the stone, revealing fully what was rising from the bag its actions had broken open, for it was as if the whole slug had been an encasing bag and the prisoner in it was now emerging. What it was was difficult, even in the light, to make out clearly, for it moved jerkily, pressed together, as if trying to hide from the lamp. Legs, yes—for one was flung suddenly aloft. A jointed leg as long as Diskan was tall, covered with a thin red skin that gleamed with shell sleekness. Then, like the slug before it, the creature gave a convulsive wriggle and straightened up.

134

Diskan heard a choked cry from Julha, a hiss out of Zimgrald. The thing was fully and fearfully clear, its elongated body poised several feet above the surface of the stone, supported on eight legs, the middle joints of which were taller than its back. There was a head, a round ball with eyes, or at least patches that resembled eyes, and a long tube it kept extending and then snapping back in a roll.

The slug had been repulsive and had stirred fear in Diskan, but looking at the thing now kicking its feet free of the shriveling skin, he knew this was a deadlier enemy. He fired.

The tube had snapped forward, a stream of liquid issuing from it. Then the searing blast caught the creature head on, and Diskan might have rayed directly into a cache of explosives, for the thing literally blew up. Scarlet flames scorched out of the midst of a sharp bark of air displacement.

Diskan staggered, blinded by the glare. He was unconscious of the pressure of a furred body against his own, shepherding him away from the edge of the drop. And the horrible smell set him gagging and choking.

"Zimgrald!" he managed to get out between gasps. "Do you see it?"

It must be dead, it had to be. But Diskan could not put aside so easily his fear that that horrible, insectival head might be still pointed at them. Why the impression of danger had been so intense he could not tell, but that they had escaped something far worse than any other danger on Mimir, Diskan was certain.

"Nothing—there is nothing—" Even the Zacathan sounded badly shaken.

Diskan rubbed his smarting eyes; he could see a little now. But to believe what his eyes reported—that was something else. Where that menace had been, entangled in the wrinkled folds of slit slug skin, there was, as Zimgrald had reported, nothing. Both slug and what had come out of it might never have been! The stone was bare.

"Did—did we just imagine it?" Diskan stammered.

The lamp beam moved. Now a slick smear caught in it, glossy in the light. Where the slug had spat at them, the trace of that remained. No, they had not dreamed it. But the bewildering effect of that last shot dazed Diskan.

"We did not imagine that—or that!"

Far back along the road they had come was a short cry.

The fireworks must have put the Jacks on their trail. The Mimiran animal was already padding on, over the battleground so strangely vacated. Diskan took the rear guard again. Zimgrald switched off the lamp and with Julha trotted after the furred one.

Diskan shouldered his pack and held the butt of his weapon close to his eyes, striving to read the amount of blaster charge remaining. Zero! He tapped it with an anxious finger, trying to make the indicator shift, but it remained the same. He restored the now useless weapon to his belt and brought out the stunner, though what use that might be against another transforming slug he did not know.

The knowledge that the hunt was now behind kept them going along that endless ridge of stone. Then the Zacathan called softly, "We are descending!"

That was true, and they had to watch their footing carefully as the thick patches of slime again splotched their way. But at last they were down, to be fronted by a wall with swamp water and growths all about it. The furred one turned to the right again, leading them to what Diskan could see only as a blank barrier. Then—it disappeared! He did not slack speed as he saw Zimgrald and the girl do likewise. In turn, he reached the slit giving into a passage running between an inner wall and an outer one. Here was no light at all, and he blundered on, knowing their full trust rested on the furred one.

It was very narrow, that passage. Diskan's shoulders brushed the chill wall on either side, and sometimes did more than brush, so he must turn sidewise to edge through. The warmth of the marsh was gone; the cold he had known outside on Mimir was biting.

"Another turn here, to the right—" Zimgrald warned him from ahead.

Diskan's outthrust hand saved him from coming up against a dead end, and he wriggled into that second runway. But there was a faint patch of light ahead, and the outlines of the rest of the party showed against it.

On they went until that gray brightened into a hint of sunlight, and at last they came out in the open with the crisp air about them. Zimgrald leaned against a block of stone. Both his hands were pressed to his bandaged body, and he breathed in heavy gasps. There was no doubting that the Zacathan was close to the end of his ability to keep going. What they needed now was a hiding place, and surely somewhere in the ruins of the city they could find that!

But, were they in the city? Diskan looked around, striving to find some landmark. The black bulk of the ruins was there, but now about them—between that and their present perch—was a stretch of blue mud-spotted marsh. Before them a kind of causeway, rough and broken, ran to a ridge. The same ridge that had brought them to Xcothal? Diskan could not be sure of that. They might have gone clear through the city and come out on the other side for all he knew. But the ridge, if they could reach it, promised some form of shelter. And the square of stone on which they stood under the whip of the wind was not a place to linger.

"We have to keep going—" Diskan moved to Zimgrald's side.

Julha half supported the Zacathan. She looked at Diskan with hostility. "He cannot!" she retorted. "Do you want to kill him?"

"I don't," Diskan replied shortly. "But this wind could—or those after us. We have to get up there"—he pointed to the ridge—"and as fast as we can."

The Zacathan nodded. "He speaks the truth, little one. And I am not finished yet!"

But he was close to it, Diskan knew, and that causeway was no easy path. He put the stunner away to leave both hands free and stepped forward, drawing the alien's arm about his shoulders.

"Down here." Diskan half carried Zimgrald to what looked the easiest way. "Keep right behind me," he flung at the girl. And those were the last sounds he made, except grunts, during that grueling journey. For once, the body hardened by years of labor did not fail him with awkwardness. He went slowly, but he made no missteps, and he moved Zimgrald along, even when more and more of the alien's weight sagged against him.

The trick was, Diskan speedily learned, to keep your eyes on the space immediately before you, to shove out of your mind all thought of the length of the track ahead or that at any moment the Jacks might explode onto the platform behind you, with you providing a fine target for a stunner—to freeze you until the enemy could collect you at their leisure. No, Jacks must be pushed totally out of mind, and the world *had* to narrow to the steps just ahead.

He was breathing heavily now, Zimgrald a dead weight. Under Diskan's ribs was a band of pain; his legs and back ached— Push that out of mind, too. Now, up the stone—there— Here was smoother walking. Now, up the next one—two strides—up the next step— Steps? Diskan's memory moved sluggishly. For the first time he allowed himself to look farther than the footing immediately ahead.

Rocks all around, and there was a line of steps before them—two, three—before another smooth stretch. They had reached the ridge!

FOURTEEN

"In here!"

Dimly Diskan saw the girl waving vigorously up ahead. He staggered on, the pain under his ribs eating him, Zimgrald's weight almost more than he could support. Once more he made the effort and brought them up and between two rock pillars into a pocket where the wind did not reach and where Julha was brushing out the drifted snow.

He tried to lower the Zacathan to the ground but stumbled and fell with his burden, the alien sprawling half over him. Then for a time Diskan simply lay until jerks at his arm brought him back to a greater degree of consciousness. Julha leaned over him. Her eyes were fierce, as hating, he thought dully, as they had been at their first meeting.

"Get up! You must get up and help me! He is worse—help me!" She slapped Diskan's face with force enough to rock his head painfully against the frozen earth. Then her fingers hooked in the hood of the parka as she tried to tug him up.

Somehow he got his arms under him and braced his body off the ground, but the effort left him panting. He rolled back against the cold rock and blinked stupidly at the frantic girl.

The Zacathan now lay on his back with a plasta-blanket from one of the packs pulled up about him. His beak-sharp nose jutted out from a face where most

139

of the flesh seemed to have melted away, so that the bone structure was sharply defined. His eyes were closed, and he was breathing through his mouth in small gasps.

Close beside him was one of the hand-port heat units—and its broadcast, though aimed directly at the Zacathan, also reached to Diskan, so that, half unconsciously, he moved his stiff hands into that welcome warmth. The pack the girl had carried and his own were open, their contents strewn around as if she had plundered both in a hurried attempt to find what she needed. And a medic-aid container was there.

"I tell you"—her hands were at her mouth, her eyes very large and fixed—"he is worse! I have no more Sustain. And he needs Deep Sleep and build shots. I don't have them!"

Diskan continued to blink. The warmth and the drugging fatigue, which made every movement an effort almost too great to bear, put a hazy wall between him and Julha. He could hear her words; they made sense in a dim way, but he did not care. He wanted to slip down, to let his leaden eyelids close, to just rest, rest—

The sharp sting of another slap brought him part way back.

"Don't you sleep! Don't you dare sleep! I tell you—he'll die unless he has help. We have to find it for him!"

"Where?" Diskan got out that one word dully.

"That cache—you said there was a survivor cache. There would be medic supplies there, all kinds. Where's the cache?" Her hands clutched the breast of the parka. She shook Diskan.

Cache? For a second the mist cleared from Diskan's fogged mind. He remembered the cache. There had been a lot of things there. Yes, there could have been a medic kit; he had not been looking for one when he explored. But the cache—he had no idea where that was now or where they were either.

He reached out, scraped up snow from a rock hollow, and rubbed it across his face. The chill of that on his skin brought him further awake.

"Where is the cache?" Her impatience needled him.

"I don't know. I don't even know whether we are on the right ridge or not."

"Right ridge?"

"We may have gone completely under the city and come up on the other side. If that's true—"

She sat back on her heels, her expression very bleak. "If that is true, he has no chance at all, has he?" Reaching out, she drew the blanket closer about the Zacathan's throat. "But you aren't sure of that?"

"No."

"Then make sure! Get up and make sure!"

Diskan grimaced. "Have you a packet full of miracles to shake out for us? I don't know this territory at all. It could take days of exploring to find out where we are. And, frankly, I can't get on my feet—not right now."

"Then I will!" She jumped to her feet, only to sway and catch at one of the rocks. She clung there, and her eyes filled, the tears slipping out to make runnels down her face.

"To collapse when he needs you?" Somehow Diskan summoned sense enough to point out to her what should already have been obvious. "We can do nothing, either of us, until we have rest, food— That may be hard for you to accept, but it is the truth."

Julha turned her head away and wiped at her cheeks with the back of her hand.

"All right!" But her agreement was delivered like a curse. "All right!"

On her knees again, she rummaged among the packs until she had found the ration tubes. One she tossed in Diskan's general direction, and he eyed it for several long seconds until he could muster enough strength to reach for it. Then he held it a space longer before he triggered the heat-open button. But once the tube did open and the aroma of its contents reached his nostrils, he found it easy to raise it to his lips.

It was hot, it tasted good, and it began to do its work against the haze of fatigue. When he had swallowed the last drop, Diskan looked around far more alertly. And it was only then that one thing about their improvised camp registered. One of their company was missing.

"The animal—where's the animal?" he demanded.

Julha was attempting to drip bits of the ration into Zimgrald's mouth. She shrugged impatiently.

"The animal? Oh, that has not been with us since we came across the stones to the ridge."

"Where did it go?" Why it was important to Diskan he did not know, but to learn that the furred one had left him gave him a curiously naked feeling, as if some support he had come to depend upon had been snatched away.

"I don't know. I haven't seen it since we came here. Does it matter?"

"It may, very much—"

"I don't see how."

"It brought us out of the city. It might be depended upon to help find the cache—"

"But I haven't seen it. It never came to the ridge."

Had it returned underground, Diskan wondered, considering some duty done when it had brought them into the open? And what of the Jacks on the trail behind? Julha might have been reading his thoughts, for now she said:

"The Jacks—what if they come here? We can't move him—"

Diskan brought out the stunner.

"The blaster charge is exhausted, and this is just about gone, too. But it is all we have. Let's see—"

Somehow he was able to pull to his feet and make a slow inspection of their present hole-up. He had to admit the girl had chosen well when she had guided him into it. There was only one entrance, a narrow slit that could be defended forever if one had proper weapons. And while the space was open to the sky now graying into dusk, the rocky walls were twice his height.

He lurched to the entranceway. The rock outside was bare, which stilled his fear of tracks. What snow Julha had brushed from the pocket had been spread away by the wind. They need not have a fire with the porto-heat unit. Yes, there was a good chance that in the night they would escape notice by any trailers.

"Listen!" He swung around. "I have the device they could have used to track you. What about Zimgrald. Can they now have one on him?"

"Not unless he wished it. I checked with Zimgrald, and Zacathans broadcast on another beam; their personality pickups can be intentionally scrambled, ours cannot. He scrambled his as soon as we knew what was happening."

Diskan was grateful for that information. The Jacks no longer had the girl's device; they had none tuned to him and none for the Zacathan—which meant they would have to do any tracking on the same level as a primitive hunter. And night was coming fast. Diskan did not believe that the Jacks would risk a scramble through this wilderness of rocks in the dark. He said as much to Julha.

"So we may be safe from *them*," she countered, "but the High One must have help!"

"There is nothing we can do tonight. A fall here could mean broken bones, and injuries for either of us would be fatal. In the morning I'll climb to higher ground and scout. If I can sight any landmarks I know and we are on the ridge land of the cache, than we can make plans."

She eyed him levelly and then picked up the stunner. "Well enough, or—not well, but what must serve. Do you sleep for a while; then I shall—"

Diskan wanted to protest, but common sense told him she was right. In his present state, he would fall asleep on watch. So he lay down in the heat of the beam near Zimgrald and was alseep even as his head turned on the ground.

143

When he roused again, with Julha tugging at him, there were no moons racing across the sky but a heavy roofing of clouds from which snow fell. The flakes hissed into drops on the warmed stones and ran in small streamlets down the rocks.

"How is he?" Diskan leaned close above the Zacathan. The shallow, gusty breathing continued. To his eyes, there had been no change in the alien's condition.

"He is alive," Julha said thinly. "And as long as he lives, there is hope. When he grows restless, put a little snow in his mouth. It seems to give him relief." She pulled the hood of her suit up and settled down beside the Zacathan.

Diskan held the stunner she had passed to him, watching the falling snow. If this was the beginning of a really bad storm, they might find themselves prisoners in this rock cleft in the morning. And yet Zimgrald manifestly could not last much longer without aid, aid that might or might not be found in the cache.

It was apparent that the Jack ship had returned—or had it? The party that had hunted them through Xcothal might have been left here to make sure of Zimgrald and the girl. If so, then the cache was for their convenience. But then Diskan did not understand the need for the broadcast that had guided him there. It certainly seemed that it had been set to toll in strangers. Who? Any of the archaeological expedition who had escaped the initial attack of the Jacks, as had Julha and Zimgrald? Or had the Jack ship, plus the spacer they had taken over from Zimgrald's people, both lifted so swiftly they had not been able to pick up all of the Jack crew planetside?

In any event, now that cache could well be the bait for a trap. The Jacks would expect desperate survivors to make a try for it. Thus, there was no chance at all for him to do as Julha wanted, to get in and out with medical supplies, escaping all detection. On the other hand, his thoughts flinched away from that alternative —that they must sit here and watch the Zacathan die, knowing all the time that there was a chance they were too prudent to take.

Diskan knew that there would be no arguing with Julha. Either he would make the try or she would. Of course, they might be so far from the right ridge that there would be no question of locating the cache at all. Diskan stood up, made one of his periodic tramps to the cleft entrance, and stared out into the dark—not because he expected to see anything there but because the action kept him awake and alert.

When he came back to the circle of heat by the unit, there was a small movement from where the Zacathan lay, and Diskan hurried to him. The alien's eyes were open and his lips moved. Hurriedly Diskan scooped up snow and strove to put it in Zimgrald's mouth. He did that three times before the Zacathan turned his head, refusing more.

"Julha?" The whisper was very faint.

"She is asleep," Diskan whispered back.

"Good. Listen carefully—" The labor of that speech was so intense that Diskan shared it vicariously. "I am—going—to —will—hibernation. I am very weak—so this may be self-killing—but it is—one—way—"

Hibernation? Diskan did not know what the Zacathan meant, but he dared not interrupt with any question.

"In my belt—" Zimgrald's hand moved under the blanket. "Get—mirror—"

Trying not to disturb the covering, Diskan felt under it. His hand was caught by taloned fingers and guided to a belt pocket. He brought out an oval of yellow metal so highly polished that even in the very faint light of the unit he could see it was a mirror.

"Julha—tell her—hibernation. Take care—"

"Yes?"

"The animals—they—have—the—secret— Open—a door—to them—if you can. Now—hold the mirror—"

Zimgrald must be slipping into delirium, Diskan thought, but obediently he held the mirror up before the Zacathan's eyes. The alien's gaze fastened on the surface of that oval in an unblinking stare. Time

145

passed, the snow hissed down, and still those eyes held upon the mirror. Diskan's fingers cramped and then his arm. He must move!

Very slowly he attempted to change his position without lowering his hand. And as if that slight movement on his part had been a signal, Zimgrald's eyelids dropped, closed. The gusty breathing stilled—

Startled and frightened, Diskan touched the Zacathan's cheek. The flesh seemed as cold as his fingers. Dead! Had Zimgrald died as he sat watching? Diskan dropped the mirror, and the metal rapped against the top of the heat unit.

"What is it?" Julha sat up. She gave a little cry and bent over the alien. "Dead! You let him die—"

"No!" He tried to find words of explanation, of the right kind to pierce the fury he could sense was growing within her. "He told me to get this"—he picked up the metal mirror and held it out to her—"said he wanted hibernation—"

"Hibernation! Oh, no—no!" Swiftly Julha stripped back the blanket and felt the arching chest three-quarters covered by the plasta bandages. "But he did—he's gone into willed sleep! And nothing prepared, nothing!"

"What is it?" Diskan asked.

"The Zacathans—they can self-hypnotize themselves into trances for indefinite periods. But it is a great strain, and with his strength already so depleted— Why did you let him do it?"

Diskan arose. "Do you think my refusal would have stopped him? I do not read him as being of less will than either of us. How long will he remain like this?"

"Until he is brought out of it. But"—she tucked the covering back around Zimgrald—"perhaps it is better so. In the trance he knows no pain or ill. And when you return from the cache with what he needs—then we can rouse him." Diskan guessed that doubts of doing that successfully were very strong in her.

"Yes, the cache—"

If they could find the cache, *if* they could find it

unoccupied, *if* the supplies there contained what they needed, *if* it was not a trap—all the ifs that had occurred to him during his time of sentry-go overloaded the scales against them. Diskan had as little hope of carrying through such an expedition as Julha had of ever rousing the Zacathan.

She was busy now attempting to roll the alien's body more tightly into the blanket and spoke to Diskan impatiently.

"Help me! He must be kept warm while he is in trance."

When that was accomplished to her satisfaction and the unit set closer to a body that, as far as Diskan could tell, was that of a dead man, she began repacking their supplies.

The sky was gray, and the snow had ceased to fall so heavily. Diskan knew that he must satisfy her with some move.

"I'll go upslope," he said. "We ought to know more about the country before we make any definite plans—"

"I'll stay here. The wrapping, the heat must not fail. I'll tend the High One until you return. You see"—she hesitated and then continued—"there is a kin-debt between us. He took sire-oath for me before my birth, for my father was once his assistant and killed on one of his expeditions. Thus, Zimgrald came to my mother and offered her the protection of his house under sire-oath. She accepted, so I became a hatchling of his line. Always has he been as my father—though he is counted as a very great personage. And it was my good fortune to be able to serve him on this venture —the first time I have been able to offer him anything in return for all he had done for me. Thus, I cannot let him die—we are kin by the bonds of the heart if not the body." She spoke as if she recited aloud her thoughts, and Diskan believed in the truth of what she said.

"Keep this!" He held out the stunner. "I'm going up now—"

He squeezed through the cleft entrance and climbed

the slope, avoiding all the snow patches he could. The light was better, and by the time he reached the top, he could see enough to give him bearings. It all depended upon this ridge's position in relation to the city.

The pull to the heights was not easy, and it took longer than he expected. But at last Diskan lay belly down on the crest of a small spur and surveyed the marshlands. There was the city, endless blocks swallowed up by a haze. He could see the causeway that had brought them to solid land. Along that nothing moved, though the black and white birds drifted in the sky over the rocky ridge land.

Slowly studying each few feet of the country as carefully as he could, Diskan turned. Then—that was it! The wide stairway down which he and the wounded furred one had come after their battle in the pass! This *was* the same ridge land—they had that one small advantage! And to his right, somewhere back in the saw-toothed ranges, was the cache. Against all good reason he was going to try to reach it. Julha would give him no other choice.

FIFTEEN

"The right ridge!" Julha's eyes glowed; she was transformed. "Then we can do it—save the High One. But you must hurry—"

Diskan knew she would not accept any argument now. In her mind, she had skipped over or pushed aside all possible dangers. In her mind, he had only to take a short walk, collect what they needed, and hasten back. If it were only that simple! But Diskan did not believe he could convince her that there were real dangers to be faced.

He tried to think of the few small things that did ride on their side of the balance. He had the parka taken from the cache; he was not wearing a protecto-suit, which the archaeologists used as a uniform. Thus, unless the Jacks really knew about him, which he doubted, he could pass for one of their company at a distance. And the cache had not been sealed. If he could cover the country between here and there by day, try to raid the cache at night— But it was with no real hope of success that Diskan made those vague plans.

Picking up one of the supply tubes, he put it in the front of his parka. The stunner rested on top of the bag. For a long moment, Diskan considered taking it. Then, regretfully, he knew that he must leave the weapon for Julha, that he could not deprive her and the unconscious Zacathan of that one small means of defense.

"Are you going now?"

He read only impatience in that.

"Yes. If I'm not back in a couple of days—"

"*Days!*" She caught him up.

"Yes—*days*. I can't jet across this ridge, remember? If I'm not back—do the best you can for yourself," he ended bleakly, knowing that to the girl he existed only as a means of aiding Zimgrald. It would be—be warming somehow if she could spare just a little thought for him. Outside the crevice, the day was dreary, and the snow came in gusts. Here was a pocket of warmth, but what was more, companionship, the knowledge that his own kind existed. His own kind? When had he ever been one with any—human or alien? Julha only gave him the same treatment now that he had always received. He was strength—to be used without thought.

Diskan scowled and made for the crack entrance—to face bared teeth, to hear a warning growl. The furred one was back, blocking that exit, though it did not appear to do more than warn. As Diskan persisted, it retreated before him, still growling, its whole stance a threat.

He came fully out of the crevice. The furred one crouched on the ground, its whip of a tail lashing, as it snarled and hissed. Yet Diskan was certain that its anger was not directed at him but at his actions. He took another step. The animal leaped, strking against him with enough force to send him staggering back against a rock, but those fangs did not snap. On the ground again it crouched, ready for another spring.

"No!"

The furred one stiffened, then fell, only its eyes alive and watching him with such intensity of purpose that Diskan was more than a little alarmed. Julha had followed him out; now she lowered the stunner she had used.

"Go on! I used only a small charge, so go quickly!"

What if the creature had been trying to warn him against some danger? Diskan climbed a point of stand-
150

ing stone and looked around. He could see the dark line of tracks where the furred one had come from the marsh below. But, save for the birds, nothing stirred there.

"Go on!" Julha's voice rose. Her arm was out, her hand raised as if she would push him away.

Diskan jumped down and caught up the helpless animal, now a limp weight in his arms.

"What are you doing?" the girl demanded harshly.

"I'm not leaving it here to freeze," he told her bluntly. "It guided us out of that place—"

"But it attacked you just now!"

"It tried to keep me from going out. It didn't use either teeth or claws. You let it stay here, understand?" For the first time, Diskan barked a direct order at her as he put the furred one down in the hollow of the crevice not too far from the Zacathan, where the heat would keep the immobile creature from the cold. Then, without another word, he went out, to begin the climb upslope for the second time.

It was a long day and a hard one. Diskan did not sight any living thing to share the white and gray world, save one or two flights of birds, high in the sky over the marsh. There were tracks in the snow but none he could identify as belonging to the furred ones, and certainly none of them were made by off-world boots. However, he kept to cover and crossed bare rock with the caution of one who has hunters sniffing at his trail.

In the later afternoon, he studied the valley of the cache from a concealed vantage point. Nosing into the sky was a ship. In lines it was not too far different from the slim government spacers Diskan had seen many times. But there was no Service insignia above the door hatch. That was closed only by the inner door, and the long tongue of the entrance ramp was out, its lower end on the soil.

Not too large a ship. Diskan tried to estimate the number that might make up its crew, but he knew little of ships, and the Jacks might put cargo space to use for extra fighting men. The best thing was not to guess at all, just be prepared for the worst.

One thing—the broadcast of the cache beam no longer sounded. It could even be that, having returned, the Jacks had dismantled that entirely. He could not be sure until he circled to that side of the valley. And the coming dusk would give him protection for that maneuver.

The impossibility of any success was like a dead weight on his shoulders, a cloud over his thinking. Diskan had never been the quick-witted improviser, and he had no hopes of suddenly developing any such ability now. The only course before him was to move along the valley wall and see what *did* wait to be faced in or about the cache.

If he had been cautious before, Diskan now became so tense that he fell twice, both times lying for long moments, fearing he did not know just what. Everytime he dared look at the spacer, there was no change, no sign of activity about the ship. Snow had drifted about the foot of the ramp—filling in shallow depressions that must mark footprints, leading off in the general direction of the cache. If snow gathered about there without melting, the ship had planeted long enough ago to let the ground cool from the deter rocket blasts.

Twilight drew in, and Diskan put on more speed. The rough footing was too difficult to cross in the dark. But the snow was falling again, and if he could get down to the level of the valley floor, it might cloak his movements. Somehow he made that descent. There were no lights showing. Perhaps the invaders were in their ship, or they might be roaming Xcothal. Diskan devoutly hoped that the latter was so.

He was able to sight the glow of the cache walls—so it had not been dismantled. But this was now a case of extracting an egg's contents without cracking the outer shell. If the bubble structure had occupants and he walked in on them— The whole expedition was hopeless. But squatting here behind a bush, with the snow plastering him and the wind slowly congealing flesh and blood, was no answer either. Something stubborn within Diskan would not accept retreat.

So he slunk around the cache, approaching it in a gradually narrowing circle. No tracks—so no one had come recently. Probably he could walk right up and in— His feet were growing numb—these boots, stout as they had seemed when he began this venture, were not made for tramping through snowdrifts. And his fingers were so cold that he held them in his armpits to bring back a feeling of life.

Now he was opposite the door. He put out one of those cold hands, touching the bubble surface, ready to activate the lock.

"Jav tiltmi's lure—?"

The snow had muffled the sound of any advance. Diskan started with shock; then a hand caught his shoulder. The speaker was level with him. The shock that had momentarily stunned Diskan's thinking processes held just a fraction too long. He tried to spin out of that hold but instead was thrown forward by an impatient shove, going on through the now opened door into the lighted interior of the cache.

Too late—there were two men there, both facing him. Diskan jerked back, to come up against the one who had pushed him in. He was too slow and clumsy. Before his poorly aimed blow got home, the other struck, with sure science. And the lights, the room, the world, vanished for Diskan.

He was floating on a sea, easily, contentedly. There was a murmur of sound somewhere, at first lulling, part of the soothing rock of the waves. Then there was a ripple of uneasiness that troubled his content, shook him. Words—someone was talking. And it was very important that Diskan learn what those words meant, who was talking. He began to concentrate, with an effort that was difficult to maintain, to separate one word from another.

"—landed in a mud bog and sank. I came ashore—on the rocks. It was very cold and it was nighttime.

153

There was a fire, where the ship crashed, before it rolled into the mud—"

That—that was the way it had been! The spacer crashing—and he had come ashore on the rocks, watched the fire and wanted its heat. It had been like that! He was Diskan Fentress who had run from Vaanchard by a stolen tape and had landed on Mimir. But who knew all this? For the voice was going on, detailing all that had happened—not only all that had happened but also what had been in his mind at the time. And who knew that? Diskan Fentress knew. The uneasy ripple was now a sharp stab of fear. That was *his* voice, going on and on, talking in that swift gabble, without his mind or will, only his memory dictating the words.

But how could that be? He was not willing that run of words. In fact, his mind was listening, not speaking. He could not define the process any better than that.

A babbler! He was either under the influence of a babbler device or some drug that worked in a similar way! And he would continue to follow the past in detail for anyone listening—without the power to delete a single experience of the past few days. Which meant that those listeners who had put him under would learn of the escape from Xcothal and the place where Julha and Zimgrald now were—as well as if he took the enemy by the hand and led them directly to the right spot. They might accept a running report, without demanding too much in the way of detail, on his early experiences on Mimir. But Diskan did not doubt they would take him through the ruins step by step, and the drug or machine would bring to the surface of his memory details so trivial that he had not even realized he had noted them at the time. There was nothing he could do about it—nothing! He would have to lie here helplessly and hear himself betray those who counted on him.

The monotone of the voice continued, not seeming in the least to belong to *him,* and Diskan tried to think. He was as much controlled as the robot watcher had been back at the space port—until that watcher had been short-circuited.

Diskan thought of his fingers. Move—move, fingers! If he could move them, then there might be hope of— But his body did not obey any command he sent. He could not even raise his eyelids to see where he lay, who listened to his babbling speech.

It was no use—they had him! They could use him to the full, and after that it would not matter in the least what they finally did with him. The despair sent his mind reeling, seeking complete unconsciousness and oblivion.

But Diskan was not to reach that welcome blackout for which he strained. Instead, he once more became aware of his words, and they were such as to deliver a counter shock.

"—the natives guided me north. They have a settlement well beyond the ruins. Aliens, but can be reached by alpha power—"

But that was nonsense—natives? The furred ones? They had no settlement that he knew of. And what was alpha power? This was no memory of his, disclosed by a babbler. Completely confused, Diskan listened as intently as he could.

"Readily accessible, willing to make contact. They know the ruins but consider them taboo. However, they will not object to off-worlders visiting there, since they believe that any curse will fall on the intruders, not on them."

"Treasure." Another voice, faint but audible. "What about the treasure?"

"Natives have traditions of two rich burial sites. Asked me if I was among those who strove to disturb the Elders. Said that such would bring upon themselves the wrath of the shadows, but that was not their concern. The places are in the city—under the center tower. Showed me from the outside. You go—"

Directions, detailed directions, for reaching the hub of Xcothal and a place within the tower. But that part

155

of Diskan's mind now listening and alert had no memory of all this.

"And the archaeologists, what of them? Have you seen them?"

"The natives spoke of them, said that the Shadows swallowed them up. They defied the guards set by the Elders. There is no need to defend what lies there, the natives say; the city can take care of its own, how the natives do not know."

"All right. He's given us what we need. Bring him out of it, now!"

What they did Diskan did not know, but there was a click somewhere within his mind, as if one intricate piece of machinery was brought into place against another. He opened his eyes and looked up at the two men watching him. Neither one was a racial or planet type Diskan could recognize. The skin of one had a blue tinge, and his coarse, brindled hair grew down in a sharp point until it almost met his bushy brows. He wore a space officer's undress coverall and had a blaster prominently belted about him.

The other had on a well-cut, well-fitting travel tunic, breeches, and boots of an inner system man. He was something of a fop, following the latest fads, for his skull had been completely denuded of hair and the bare skin tatooed with an intricate design, which a filigree skull cap of gold emphasized. Diskan had seen his like at the space ports, a Veep from some decadent trade world, but to see such a man here was a surprise. His type was as much out of place on Mimir as Diskan had been on Vaanchard. Now he smiled, though the goodwill suggested by that stretch of thin and colorless lips did not reach, nor was it intended to reach, his slightly protruding eyes.

"We have to thank you, Fentress. And your report has cleared one minor mystery, as to why the tape we were at such pains to obtain from your father's collection was so far wrong as a guide. Luckily, we tested it before taking off; otherwise, we might have lost a vast amount of highly valuable time.

156

"You *have* cost us some of that essential time, young man. But tonight you have given us that which makes up for such delays. You realize that we have had you babbling?"

Diskan nodded. He was still trying to take stock of the situation. There was a third man present, wearing inner system dress, but of a less elegant cut. A medic's symbol on his tunic meant he must be the private medic of the Veep; perhaps his drugs had provided the babble.

"Good. We had thought to learn a rather different story from you. But that is not important now. These natives, you say they will not oppose entrance to the city.

"Yes," Diskan improvised.

"These planet taboos are sometimes helpful then. A lucky situation. They are willing to let us provoke any curse and are so not inclined to prevent exploration."

"A trap, Gentle Homo? They might have planted such a tale," broke in the medic.

"Of course. But we need not spring any trap ourselves, need we? We have those who can do it for us, including our young friend here—unless, of course, he *wants* to be reprocessed in some correction lab. And do not believe that I shall hesitate in turning you over to the authorities to do just that, Fentress, unless you agree to be sensible. Your flight from Vaanchard puts you directly into the 'unreliable personality' grouping, and you can be given to the Patrol whenever I choose, with a cover story locked into your memory pattern to satisfy our purposes. It is always best to get on a footing of complete understanding at once, isn't it?"

Diskan knew very little of what could be done to a man's brain. What this Veep threatened could be possible. They might be able to plant false memories, just as they had been able to make him babble, ship him off Mimir, and turn him over to the Patrol as an escaped criminal. Only, they thought he had really babbled, that they knew the truth of what had happened to him here, and they did not! What had fed all

157

the false information through his lips? These "natives" —the furred ones? He could only take action now as it came and wait for an explanation.

"All right." He had hesitated before giving that agreement, but perhaps that was natural. Apparently the pause raised no doubts in the Veep.

"Yes, of course you will cooperate, all we need you to. Now I suggest a period of rest; we need not begin our expedition until tomorrow. You, young man, will remain where you are. If you wish to escape undue fatigue, accept my word that you are under muscle lock stass and that beam will not be lifted until we are ready for you to move. To try to raise so much as one finger will be a failure. Scathr nur gloz—" He switched from Basic to another tongue and picked up a fur-lined cloak, shrugging it about his shoulders, pulling a visored hood up to cover his head and most of his face. The medic did the same, and they passed out of the range of Diskan's vision.

The blue-skinned space officer came a few steps closer to stand over the prisoner. With one boot he toed Diskan, whose body moved stiffly as if all joints were locked into place.

"You babbled, you swamp worm." He spoke thoughtfully. "And loose babble cannot be faked. But these natives—we didn't see any. How come you found them so neat—like you were in a straight entry orbit?"

"They found me—" Again Diskan improvised.

"And maybe they're going to find us." The Jack's hand went to the butt of his blaster. "Let us hope they keep to this 'you blast your way and I'll blast mine' policy. If they don't, there may be some blasting they won't like. And you could just be in the middle if we come up against any cross—"

He toed Diskan again and then went off, leaving the prisoner with a frustrating collection of unanswered questions.

SIXTEEN

Diskan lay immobile, his eyes closed but his mind very busy. They had had him babbling, and he had talked all right, but some of that information had been false. And he still could not understand how that had happened or from where that information had flowed, seemingly to convince his captors. The "natives" —who? He was certain he was being used to funnel the Jacks into Xcothal; that was apparent. But this business of the curse and the city that had its own defenses—which the Jacks would dismiss as superstition.

And the Veep here— What *did* the Jack believe lay hidden on Mimir—something so rich as to attract backing from an inner system grandee, actually bring him to share the operation? But perhaps he thought his pirate employees would develop sticky fingers if not right under his eye. What Julha and Zimgrald had told Diskan made sense, that the Zacathan's name was associated with two famous archeaological finds in the past, thus making his presence on Mimir a gamble good enough to draw an ordinary Jack raid—but not this setup under a Veep! Such a man could back a grab, but to come along himself meant so big a haul as to be worth the risk.

That reference to the tape from his father's collection. Was it the tape he had seen Drustans take from the rack? But Diskan could not accept that his father, or the Vaans, had had a part in any Jack grab. Diskan tried to remember who else had been there that night. A Zacathan from the embassy, a Free Trader, and there had been other off-world guests. But he had paid so little attention to any of them, had been so buried in his own hole of misery, that they had been only fleeting faces to which he could not now set names. And Drustans' connection with any one of them? No answers there.

But one thing Diskan did know—with the Veep in the open this way, his own life, and that of any witness, was no longer worth a puff of breath once his usefulness was over. The Veep might talk of having Diskan in a vice because of his flight from Vaanchard and the stolen spacer, but a dead man was even easier to control. He could be simply left anywhere on this planet; if found later, he would be accepted as an unfortunate survivor from a wreck. And Zimgrald and Julha, if they were located by these, could expect no other fate either. Perhaps already all the rest of the archaeological expedition's personnel were dead.

For the moment, and a very short moment that might be, the Zacathan and the girl were safe. Diskan had not babbled about them, thanks to the false information for which there was no sane accounting. The Jacks would probably head for the city in the morning, using him and the other hostages they had mentioned as shields to test any trap in Xcothal. And in the open, he might have a chance for escape, if a very slim one.

Natives? His thoughts kept circling back to that. The furred ones—it could only be the furred ones. And there was one way—Diskan shrank from that; he would have shivered had such motion been possible to his stass-locked body. This was far more difficult than that climb up the unstable cliff, the march across the underground bog, the fight with the slug thing, the carrying of Zimgrald to the ridge. Diskan had never feared so much the risking of his body, but this meant the risking of something else, a part of him he did not want to gamble. Yet, twist and turn though his thoughts did, they always returned to one solution, probably the only one.

Diskan at last faced the truth of that and made himself accept it. Then, before panic swept away all courage, he did it. The lame furred one, he concentrated on that one, building up in his mind the clearest picture he could mentally paint of the furred body, those compelling eyes, as he had seen the Mimiran animal last, before Julha had struck it down with the stunner. Surely the effects of that ray had worn off now, and it never dulled the mind when used on a low-charge.

In that mental picture, the furred one's eyes grew larger and larger, flowed together to form a great dark pool or tunnel or space into which Diskan was drawn, faster and faster, whirling in, spinning around.

He could not break away now because he was not summoning the other, as he had summoned animals on Nyborg, the varch on Vaanchard, but was being summoned instead. And that feeling of utter helplessness in the grip of relentless power was so terrible that he was absorbed instantly in a battle to keep some rags of his identity, not to be diffused in a darkness where Diskan Fentress would cease utterly to exist.

The dizzying whirl *could* be fought, he discovered. He was still himself, a small hard core of man. Content to keep that, he relaxed a small portion of his resistance. Now it was like hearing himself babble, having no control over either words or the memory that produced them. Communication was in progress all about him. He could catch a word, a thought, tantalizing in its almost intelligibility, but never enough to make sense. Babble—could this have been the influence that had so skillfully planted the false information in his mind?

A feeling of growing impatience. He shrank from that. This was the old sickening frustration of being the one completely out of step, of being trapped in a round of stupid action when mind and body did not mesh. But to his loss of confidence there was this time a prompt response, an understanding that amazed Diskan. And there clicked into his mind a picture so vividly presented that he might be viewing it with his eyes. What *were* these furred ones that they had such power?

On the last of those stone steps he had once descended to enter the bogged streets of Xcothal lay a pile of driftwood. A fire to be built and then the addition of branches to which frozen red leaves were still attached. This must be done before they entered the city. It was imperative!

Diskan assented, how he did now know. And then he was whirling again, sick and dizzy, being ejected from the dark pool of the furred one's eyes. But he brought with him something he had never known before in his life and did not realize even yet that he had, though it steadied his spirit, quickened his thinking, and was an armor against what might come. For the first time in his life, Diskan Fentress knew a kinship founded in trust.

Consciousness spoke to consciousness, picking up another mind here, there, across feet or leagues, causing a stir as wind might ripple a pool; yet this was a far more purposeful ripple.

Response, brothers, at last! A seeking to answer our seeking. Give now the power and see what is the final fashioning. We have tried this one, will try again. Perhaps at last we have a shaping to serve our needs! The uniting—ah, brothers—think upon the uniting after all this weary space of time.

And the others?

After the manner of their spirits, let them advance or retreat or be served as they would serve. The lizard one, the female, they are not for our shaping. Among these new ones—who knows—perhaps we shall find more. But there is one, this one, my brothers, who lies ready. Concentrate upon the shaping. Let the word go forth!

So he was to build a fire on that last step and add the leaves to it, Diskan mused. The furred one willed it so, and from it would come—? Then he remembered Zimgrald's last words before the Zacathan had willed himself into a trance.

"The animals have the secret—"

Diskan had thought those words born out of fever, but perhaps not. What secret? That of the treasure? What treasure? And what had the leaves to do with it? The first night when he had dreamed of the city, long before he had known that it existed in reality, he had been in the valley of the red-leaved wood, had used some of those to feed his fire, had awakened under branches that still bore them. Leaves, the spark-filled smoke—some drug to summon up the far past in a dream?

Was he being ordered to return the Jacks to the Xcothal that was? Yes, that was what the furred ones wanted. And it might just work. If he could keep his own sense and the rest of the party were drugged—! But what reason could he give his captors for building such a fire? Order of the natives before going into a sacred city? Would the Jacks or the Veep accept that? No use worrying now; he would have to take such problems as they came. With a confidence he had not known before, Diskan decided that tomorrow's action would have to be improvised and that tonight he could do nothing. As if he let go some anchorage with that, he drifted into sleep.

The next day was one of the bright, clear ones that appeared to alternate with storms on Mimir. As the party set out from the cache, to be joined at the ship by the Veep and a man wearing the badge of a personal guard, together with the medic, Diskan wondered what this world was like in a warmer season. The bogs must be twice as treacherous and the waterways bad traveling, but these valleys in the ridge-

163

land might be pleasant—not that he was ever likely to see them so!

Three Jack crewmen all well armed, the Veep and his two, and one of those a professional guard not only expert with the usual weapons but also in all the various forms of unarmed combat as well—that was their party. No wonder they had released Diskan from stass and allowed him to travel unhampered by any bonds. To try a break from such company was simple suicide.

At first, Diskan was uneasily aware of the guards at his heels, but by the time they reached the traces of the ancient road on the crest of the heights, his apparent docility had had its effect. The Jacks kept close, but they no longer watched his every movement, now giving more attention to the countryside. And a wary watch that was. The space officer's distrust of the "natives" must have been shared by his crew.

But perhaps they felt a little of what Diskan knew to be a fact. This rocky ridge was not empty of life as it had been on his return to the cache. Though he saw no paw prints in any snow patch nor caught the least hint of any scout, yet they were under observation, and many watched them on their way.

"These natives"—the Veep, cloaked and mask-hooded, moved up beside Diskan—"where is their village?"

Diskan stabbed a finger in the direction toward which they now headed. "There—"

"And they will make no trouble when we enter the ruins?"

Diskan allowed his expression to go stolid. If he had babbled long and loudly enough about events leading up to his landing on Mimir, and he must have, then the Veep would be expecting dull acceptance from him now. He had never tried to play any part, but he had only to think himself back to the days on Vaanchard and the rest would be easy. However, here was a chance to do a little preparation for future action.

"Why should they, Gentle Homo?" he asked. "It is

164

their belief that that which guards the ruins will protect itself without any aid from them. They only say that the watch fire must be built to insure that it does not issue forth from the city in its anger at being disturbed."

"A watch fire?"

Diskan knew that the eyes behind the visor of the cloak hood were measuring him with dangerous intentness. The Jack officer had one kind of cunning and the force to back his decisions. This Veep had higher and more dangerous powers of the same order. He was not a man to be easily fooled.

"A fire must be built at the entrance of the city. This is very important to them. They did it when they took me in. I think it warns off what they believe lurks there—but the fire only acts so for a space."

"And you saw nothing dangerous during that visit?"

"Only tracks—" Diskan thought of the slug paths.

"Tracks? What kind—off-worlders'?"

Diskan shook his head. The Veep had been quick to ask that. But the Jacks had been exploring in Xcothal —twice, maybe more times. Why this pretense that they had not come to the city before? And where were the other hostages the Veep had spoken of last night? Diskan almost broke step. Suppose the Veep already knew about Zimgrald and the girl and intended to pick them up now?

"Strange paths on the earth," he answered mechanically, while he imagined what might happen, "marked with slime. Some were very large—"

The Veep nodded. "Some native swamp creature, only to be suspected. But those Imbur's men have already reported. They seem to be nocturnal and need not be feared. And that was all you saw?"

"Yes," Diskan answered absently. For the past few moments, a sense of not being a prisoner alone among his enemies but a scout of another force had grown so strong that he began to fear he might betray the confidence building in him now.

"And they do not fear that this treasure will
165

be found and taken from the city, these natives?"

"It is not their concern." The words arose easily to his lips as they had when he had babbled, and Diskan let them come, content to listen himself to what might be a subtle message concealed in a spate of vague information. "They consider it a matter of the Elders, to be handled by the guards *those* set."

The Veep beat his gloved hands together as if his fingers were chilled. "Their confidence would seem excessive under the circumstances." That might be his own thoughts rather than a remark addressed to Diskan. "Of course, they may not have dealt with off-worlders before."

Diskan did not have to turn his head to know that the eyes behind the visor slits were trying to penetrate to *his* thoughts, watching for any clue as to whether Diskan knew of the archaeologists.

"I do not know—only what they told me."

"Told you?" the Veep repeated. "They speak Basic —but that would mean that they do have off-world contacts."

Diskan waited for a clue, but he dared not be silent too long. Then he replied; "They think messages—in mind pictures."

Had he been right to disclose that much truth? Nothing from the hidden watchers either assured or protested.

"Telepaths!"

Yes, the Veep could accept that. There were several known telepathic races, and, Diskan recalled with a chill at perhaps having made a bad mistake, one was the Zacathan. But he had said it and must now wait on results.

"Telepaths." The Veep was smiling now, the lips showing under the edge of the visor definitely curved. "Well, another link in the chain. No wonder the High One chose to do his hunting here with so small a party. Also, perhaps why these think they have nothing to fear from explorers in their city. Remote controls— But I am afraid, Fentress, that our ingenuity

166

can overcome even such alien preparedness. We have our defenses and offenses. Also, we shall have you and others to spring any traps."

Diskan understood the other's confidence. Every one of the party, except himself, was strung about with weapons and various devices. Some must be detection and location units. They had had those on all morning. He did not believe that either the Veep or the Jack officer would have started before taking every precaution possible to galactic science and ingenuity. Yet, they had *not* detected the watchers, and he did not believe that they knew he was in slight contact with the hidden ones. Therefore, Mimir's people did have that which could baffle off-world defenses.

"They say that the city *can* protect its own. I don't know how." Diskan tried to make his voice heavy and sullen. And perhaps he was successful, for the Veep laughed.

"No, you wouldn't, would you, Fentress? Ah, rendezvous as ordered, and right on the proper tick of time."

Three figures moved out of rock shadows into the full sunlight. One was a Jack, armed like his fellows, The other two—Diskan thought they walked with an odd jerkiness, as if each step were taken to order. But he could have shouted his relief. Neither was Zimgrald or Julha.

As the parties joined together, he got a good view of the other captives.

"Drustans!" That cry of recognition was startled out of him.

But his Vaan stepbrother was—was gone! This stranger shambling along on curiously stiffened legs, his features frozen blankly, his arms tight to his sides, as if held there by invisible bonds, was far from the lithe, graceful, supremely confident person who had increased Diskan's sense of inferiority and clumsiness every time he looked at him. And the other with Drustans—a Survey crewman by his uniform—walk-

167

ing with the same stilted gait, his face expressionless, his eyes locked on something inward—

"Yes, a family meeting." The Veep's smooth voice purred. "Unfortunately, Drustans came to know too much, so we had to bring him with us when we left Vaanchard. He had played several roles for us—that of research expert, and then hostage, and now to research again—or should we say scouting? Ah, perfect, Fentress. I think you once wished to be a First-in Scout, following in your father's orbit as it were. Well, now you are about to realize that dream, a little late. I would also advise you to note the present condition of these Gentle Homos. They caused us difficulty—at first. But now they agree perfectly to all our plans. They will carry out any order, including turning on each other—or you—should the need for drastic discipline arise. So far you have been more cooperative, Fentress. Continue to be so and you will not have to be reduced to the same type of amiability."

The other prisoners were under some form of mental stass control, Diskan decided. Perhaps the condition was by now permanent, and they were past any aid. He had heard of such induced robot compliance, though the practice was deemed worse than willful murder on any civilized planet. A threat of this was to be feared.

He went on, Drustans falling in on his left, the other prisoner on his right, their jerky pace bothering him as he tried to keep step.

"With such a foreguard," Diskan heard the Veep say, "we need have no fears."

What did the off-worlder expect? That this road was mined, that they were walking into an ambush? Did the Veep really know about the watchers and this was his answer to any menace from them?

No!

A reassurance out of nowhere, but reassurance. The watchers were free to move as they wished; the off-worlders would not see them. Ahead was the narrow pass where Diskan had fought the beast at the side of the furred one. Two of the red birds arose, flying
168

sluggishly, well fed. The stench of old death was wafted back to them. One of the space crew, blaster drawn, cut past Diskan and his companions to investigate, and then waved them on.

"Some kind of animal, dead," he reported.

"Which we do not need to be told!" snapped the Veep waspishly. "Faugh—!"

They passed the partially stripped bones. The beginning of the stairway was not much farther, and below Xcothal. At a word of command, they halted. The Veep scrambled to a higher point, using far-seeing lenses to view the ruins. Xcothal was the same today as it had been that other time, Diskan noted. Near to hand, the buildings were clear-cut against the frozen marsh, but farther out a curious haze distorted the sight. He should be able to see those higher buildings at the core, the tower of the hub, from here. Yet there was only a mist rising in the direction where he was sure they stood. He watched the Veep adjust and readjust the lenses, as if, even with those to aid him, he could not get a clear sight of the bones of Xcothal.

Diskan looked down the stair. On the wide platform of the last step, it was just as they had pictured it for him—a pile of drift waiting to be ignited. Among the yellow-white of the branches bright splotches of scarlet, the leaves—

That was his part of the action. Put flame to that and it would all begin. What was "it"? Diskan did not know, but the anticipation swiftly filling him was born of confidence and that trust he could not define.

Light the fire and then—

SEVENTEEN

The Veep had given up his survey of the city and had dropped down to join them. As he slid the lenses back into their carrying case, he looked down the giant stairway to the platform where the firewood waited. Then he glanced over his shoulder at Diskan.

"All there waiting for us—very convenient." His comment was a silky purr. "We announce our coming, and they make the arrangements to greet us. How simple do they think we are?"

"That firewood is not just for our use," Diskan returned. "They do the same when they enter the ruins. It is their custom."

"And perhaps a means of defense, Gentle Homo." The medic spoke for the first time.

"A defense for *us* to use?" The Veep laughed. "It would seem that we do have samples of simple wit among us after all."

"The smoke from the fire, Gentle Homo, might have some importance," the medic persisted. "If the natives themselves build such fires, it might be most wise to follow their example."

"Smoke?" Again the Veep laughed. "Even with the wind blowing in the right direction, how far would that smoke reach? And we have only his word that they do it—"

"Given under babbler influence," the medic retorted.

The Veep stared down at the waiting wood. "I don't see any reason for it—"

Then the Jack officer cut in. "Lots of things that don't seem reasonable to us, Gentle Homo, do to aliens. Maybe it's a rite of some sort. If so, it won't do any harm to follow it. Might bring them down on us if we didn't."

"We are grateful for your bending your past knowledge to the present problem, Murgah," the Veep replied sharply, "but I do not think we shall build any bonfires—"

Diskan tried not to let his consternation show. He was under their constant surveillance; there was no way of starting the fire—or was there? He tried to think it out, appealing dumbly to that support he had sensed during the hours of ridge travel. Contact still held; his "reach" met it. But there was no answer to his silent question. Either the furred ones could not, or would not, supply him with the next move. Diskan was on his own.

"March!" The guard behind Diskan underlined that order with a prod of blaster barrel in the small of the prisoner's back. His two stassed companions had already started to descend. They would go down that stairway, out into the ruins. He had to get the fire going—he had to!

There was one way. He was driven to it by desperation. The three of them—himself, Drustans, and the controlled Survey man—were still in the lead. There was no one between Diskan and the brushwood. He eyed the stone treads before him, counted them, tried to judge their height and from which one of them he must make his try.

They were about the fifth tread from the platform. Now—and he must make it look natural. There was no use ending up crisp in a ray without achieving his goal. It was funny. So many times in the past he had fallen over his own clumsy feet without wanting to—now he must do it on purpose! His fingers already probed under his parka. Luckily, he had been warming his hands there from time to time. This guard

171

would not suspect a familiar gesture. The latch on his belt pouch—would it never yield? Hot, burning—his fire stone was still active! That had been his one fear, or the greater one among many small ones.

In his bare hand it was a searing pain, almost as bad as the wound he had taken in his fight with the watch robot. Now!

Diskan tripped and fell forward, fighting any impulse to save balance. He landed hard on the solid stone of the platform, and the force of that drove most of the breath out of him, was a shock that brought him close to a blackout. But he held to his purpose. Roll now—he had to roll and make it look right. A moan—yes, he could moan and try to get to his feet—

Only that abortive scramble brought him instead to the pile of firewood. He flung out his arm, allowed his tortured fingers to open so that the stone fell into the central mass. Then he wavered back, his arm over his face, and allowed himself to go limp. There was a clatter of boot heels on the stone; there were cries from behind him.

But also there was a sudden crackling, a flash of heat, as if no natural fire had been laid and waiting. Diskan stole a glimpse. The whole pile was bursting into flame—it might have been soaked in some combustible chemical. And from it, spark-filled smoke arose, not straight up into the air but puffing out from the sides in clouds. The first cloud was already about him. Diskan breathed in a spicy aroma that seemed to clear his head, taking away the pain in his hand, the shock of the bruises he had taken in his fall. He saw the guard come charging into the cloud and then—

Color, light, running water, fresh and scented, rising about his legs. Xcothal streets in festival time. And with him the brothers-in-fur marching or rather weaving their joy dance around and around. Those shadows with whom he had sensed a deep oneness before, they were darker, had taken on more substance. He caught tantalizing glimpses of forms—beauty, grace, strength. If he could only see them better!

Rich fabrics hung from the windows and made soft ripples of color down the walls. And the wind about him was a gentle caress, as sweet in its scent as the water continually flowing about his tired feet, for he was tired, Diskan knew, happily tired. He had come a long and arduous journey, and this was the end of it—this was home!

Pleasure, completion—he could put no other name to the emotion that united him with the brothers-in-fur. The shadow people, they were growing more and more real; there was one walking to his left—

No—these others were not shadow people! They were men like himself—though Diskan could not make out their faces. A kind of sparkling aura wreathed about them, moving spirally about their bodies, so that he caught only glimpses of a swinging arm, wading legs. Yet he knew they were his kind. And they did not belong, like the shadow people. They were not a part of Xcothal as he was a part. No brothers-in-fur kept pace with them or wove the thal pattern between them. They were intruders!

Diskan wanted to attack, to expel them forcibly from the peace and happiness of Xcothal, but the brothers wove the thal pattern for him to walk within, and to break that was sacrilege.

In their own time, brother! The assurance came to him. *In their own time and their own way they shall be judged and dealt with. Think not of them now.*

Yet to see those dark shapes stalking along his own path spoiled his homecoming. He could not abandon mind and heart to the thal pattern as he should, and that was dangerous. The warning came from the brothers:

Drift with the thal, right, left, in and out, thus, and thus, and thus.

Though his lips did not move and no sound issued from his throat, Diskan felt as though he were singing, not words but a melody that was born of the rhythm of the thal. And as he so sang, he could hear the others—not the intruders, not even the brothers-

173

in-fur, but the shadow ones—who must become real, they must!

The water was rising higher about him; he was coming to the heart-core of Xcothal. Surely in this place the shadows would put on the robes of reality and he would be one with them as he must be. There was the tower, and from it issued the call, so that the shadows were massing there, flowing up the circular stair into *That Which Was, Had Been, and Would Ever Be!*

But the intruders were coming, too, and whenever Diskan glanced at them or thought of them, the shadows dwindled, the song dimmed, and he was not as sure of the pattern of the thal. Why must they come?

In their own way, they, too, must see—what they wish to see. And from that seeing will grow the judging. Patience, brother, patience. To all there is an end.

But not to *That Which Is!*" he protested

So do we hope, brother. Prove it so, oh, prove it so!

Diskan flinched under the force of that appeal, under the burden they had dropped upon him without warning. But what did they want of him? What must he do? He was without answers.

Do what comes to you. Act as you must, brother.

Face that which must be faced as your nature would have you.

Advice that meant nothing. His feet were on the steps now; yet still he moved in the thal pattern. Only the shadows were gone; those who moved with him were the intruders, still masked by those sparkling veils. Those and the brothers-in-fur—for he was their key! That much came to him in a flash. For long they had been locked away from their hearts' desire; on him depended their futures also. Yet when Diskan sent out a call for enlightenment, there came no answer. He understood; this action was his alone. They had given him all the aid that was theirs to give; now he walked, as did those others, to face a test and a judging.

He was in the wedge hall, but it was far different

from the way he had seen it last. There were walls of silver over which advanced and retreated, glowed and dimmed, thal patterns. And—some of those he knew!

Diskan traced with his eyes a running, twisting curl of red-gold, and then he smiled. You wrought with your thought, thus and thus, and—brilliance almost blinding. The glowing surface dripped small shining motes to cascade to the floor in a glittering pile. Material that could be used—

Treasure! These had come seeking a treasure, had they not? Glittering toys of no real value. Let them have this treasure of theirs—

Again Diskan wrought with his will. The drops—gems? It did not matter. They were toys—could be used thus—

The drops formed into a design and remained so. A diadem of crimson and gold rested on the pavement. Diskan laughed. Toys—with some beauty—made to please the eye. But that *he* could make them so—!

The flash of wonder that crossed his mind set him to act again. Treasure—let him show these others treasure such as they sought, which was in no way the treasure of Xcothal! This time he willed a belt, dripping a fringe of blue-green jewels.

Yes, yes! Do what must be done, brother. Treasure.

"But this is not the treasure!" Diskan protested. "Toys for playthings, to amuse and adorn. They are worth nothing beyond delighting the eyes for a space."

You are right to offer them to these others. Make them, brother!

Diskan obeyed, though his first exultation waned. They lay spread across the floor, what he had fashioned by his will from the energy of the thal. And they were nothing, for could not anyone amuse himself so?

Not so, brother. Now the testing—watch!

Those sparkling clouds that clung about the intruders thinned, vanished. Diskan recognized them all as memory lanced the spell of Xcothal. There they stood, the Veep, his personal guard, the medic, the three Jacks, the stassed prisoners and their Jack guard, while the color and the thal patterns receded from the walls. There was a chill, a withdrawing that Diskan felt as a pain. Even the brothers-in-fur were gone.

Only the glittering array on the floor was still the same—or was it? To Diskan's eyes the gems now had a hard, repelling glare. Had—had he really willed them out of the thal patterns or was that a dream also? Could they be real?

The Jack guarding the prisoners gave a hoarse cry and leaped forward, grabbing at a trail of necklace. He choked and crumpled up, his fingers only inches away from the prize. The Veep's guard held a stunner well to the fore, while his employer pushed back the hood of his cloak, gazing a little blankly at the wealth before him, as if he could not believe in its existence.

He stooped as if to pick up the blue-green jeweled belt and then drew back. Straightening, he turned and beckoned to the stassed Survey man.

"Get it," he ordered in a voice hardly above a whisper.

The prisoner jerked forward and stooped in turn. His fingers moved with stiff clumsiness, but he picked up the shimmering length and held it, his eyes betraying no interest. After a long moment, the Veep reached out slowly and drew it away from the captive's clutch. Back and forth it passed through his hands, a rippling glory of gem light.

There was a new expression on the Veep's face. He was plainly excited, entranced. "It's real—real I tell you!" His voice climbed to an echoing cry.

The other three Jacks looked from the massed glitter on the floor to the private guard and back again. There was avid hunger in Murgah's eyes, but he did not advance to the lure. The limp body of his man lay between as a warning.

Only the Veep's guard was intrigued, too. His long years of training and control held; he continued to watch the three Jacks on their feet, but he also stole glances at the loot.

176

"Real!" The Veep repeated, and that word hung almost visibly over them.

Diskan tensed, warned by a concentration from the unseen pointing in upon them. He shot a quick glance to his left. Drustans and the Survey man were the only two apparently oblivious of the display. The Jacks were plainly straining at the leash—and that leash was their respect for the Veep's personal guard. How long that fear of his ability would hold them in check, Diskan had no idea, but that they *would* make some move he was sure.

The Veep's first bemusement was wearing off. He ran the belt back and forth through his hands, but now he studied it critically, as if he knew some fault existed, that it merely remained for him to find it. Then he raised his eyes to Diskan.

"Where did this come from? Our scouts did not find it here earlier!"

"Look about you," Diskan replied. "This is not the same city that they visited." He expected the Veep to demand an explanation of that.

Instead, still holding the belt, the man walked back to the entrance of the wedge room. He stood outlined in the door, gazing into the open of the hub. His guard stepped back a little to give him room but still kept a position from which he could cover any advance on either the treasure or his employer. Then the Veep returned.

"You are right," he agreed in his usual controlled tone. "This is no longer a ruin. So what has happened, a time twist? Or are we now mind-controlled?"

"The smoke!" The medic broke in. "Back there—that smoke!"

The Veep shook his head impatiently. "I am drug blocked, so are you, Sherod. What is it, Fentress?"

"I don't know. But this is the real city—" He did not know why he added that.

The guard moved, edging back, his stunner still and ready, while he worked his way crab-fashion to the door as the Veep had done before him. Once there, he

177

pressed his shoulders against the wall, giving a light-ning survey outside. When he turned again, there was a shade of expression on his face for the first time.

"What is this?" he asked of the Veep, and his tone was sharp, with none of the usual diffidence.

"I have not the slightest idea. This"—the Veep waved the belt in his hand so it was a glittering whip—"feels real, looks real—and I'm blocked against any ordinary hallucination. But how much we dare depend upon our senses here and now— What about it, Sherod?"

The medic shook his head. "I did not think it could be done—such illusion fostered. They *must* be illusions—"

Murgah laughed, a harsh crackle. The blue skin about his mouth showed deep brackets. "One way to find out. We take this with us, and we leave—fast!"

"I'm inclined to agree with you, captain." The Veep nodded. "And, as an additional precaution, the har-vesting will be done by our non-friends." He gestured to Drustans, the Survey man, and Diskan. "You—gather it in!"

The Survey man was closest, and he went down on one knee to pick up the red and gold diadem. Drustans moved to the right and leaned over. Diskan's inner tension sparked. He threw himself to the floor as a crackling ray burned across the space near where he had stood. It caught the Veep's guard, and he had only an instant in which to scream.

Diskan, still rolling, was brought up against stiff legs, and Drustans fell upon him. The Vaan's arms flailed out awkwardly, and another weight came down on the two of them. Diskan, his face ground painfully against the stone, was helpless for a space to struggle free. He heard other cries of pain and smelled the overpowering odor of rayed flesh.

Grasping for a handhold to draw him free of the struggle over him, Diskan closed his hand on a sharp object and dragged it to him. Then he gave a last mighty heave and rolled the weight off him, sliding forward to the wall.

By the time he pulled around, the battle had become a hunt. Stabbing lances of fire from the door, two other rays answering from the chamber. Men ran, dodging into the open. Diskan sat up. In his hand he held a gemmed knife, which he regarded with dull surprise.

The stunned crewman was now dead. One of the rays had caught him during the melee. And not too far from him lay the Survey man, also burned. By the door huddled the Veep's guard. And two figures rolled over and over, still struggling, within arm's reach of Diskan. To all appearances, they fought in a kind of slow motion, which was almost amusing.

Of the rest who had been in that chamber, the Veep, Captain Murgah, and one of the Jacks were gone. Who hunted whom, Diskan did not know. What mattered was he was free. He got to his feet.

The fighters rolled apart. One lay on his back, his hands and feet moving as if he were still engaged in that struggle. Diskan bent over him. Drustans! How the Vaan could have put up a fight at all when stass-controlled, Diskan had no idea. Sherod lay beyond, around his neck a gem-set necklace pulled tight.

"Get—away—" There was the light of reason in Drustans' eyes now as they met Diskan's.

Diskan did not answer, but he pulled the Vaan to his feet and steadied that lighter, slender body against his own.

"Get away—out of the city!" the other insisted. He wobbled to the door and would have fallen had not Diskan caught him.

Out of the city—Diskan had left this city once before. And then, too, he had aided a wounded man—Zimgrald. Zimgrald and Julha! From faint, far-ago memories planted in a misty past, they snapped into urgent life in Diskan's mind. Zimgrald, Julha up in the rocks, with death drawing in as a dark cold—

"All right." He swung an arm about Drustans' waist and pulled the Vaan along. But it was like wading through water-washed sand in which there was no

179

stable footing. Diskan had to fight that within him which cried, "No! No!"

And he fought, though his breath came in painful sobs and he dared not look around him at the Xcothal that had been—that was now for him.

EIGHTEEN

"Let me go—for now let me go!" Diskan did not know whether he was crying that aloud or through that other way of communication. "This is what I must do!"

Abruptly, as if some decision he had not shared in had been made, that backward drag on him ceased. He was down the curved steps into the hub, Drustans staggering beside him. And the city was strange, for it wavered, as though one mist-edged picture fitted over another not quite exactly. Sometimes they stumbled between lines of dark ruins. Sometimes the water washed their feet, banners lined the walls, and the shadow folk came and went on their own mysterious business.

Would they win out of here? Diskan had tried this before and found all streets led to the same pond, but this time he went with a kind of inner certainty. Only what about the Jacks and the Veep? And those others who had been here earlier, in the ways beneath the tower? All might now be prowling these dark streets.

"Where are we going?" Drustans asked, breaking Diskan's concentration of listening, staring, seeking out what might lie hid in any darkened doorway, any side lane.

"To the ridge—if we can make it."

"You think that the natives might help?"

"They have helped—"

"You mean—the illusions?"

Illusions? No, Xcothal was no illusion, but Diskan was not going to argue that now. He was eaten by the need for speed—he must reach the fugitives hidden on the high land and then—then what? Diskan did not know what would happen after that, but that he was following a necessary sequence of action he was sure.

This time there was no befogging of the trail. Even the haze that always hung to confuse the eyes when one looked out over the ruins lifted. No more half matching of a city with its bones. Xcothal's rubble was clear in the light of the moons, that pallid light so bright that Diskan could see the many tracks breaking the white surface of the snow, tracks all leading into the city—boots and paws. The furred ones had been numerous, and they still gave him escort now, though he could not see them.

He is going from us!

In this he is right. It is what he must do—a shaping of his own kind, which is needed, a road he must walk for himself.

Brothers! For the first time Diskan tried to join in that communication which was not for voice or ear but which nonetheless existed.

For a long moment, there was no reply. Then an upsurge of clamor as if many thoughts shouted all together.

Brother! And the joy in that was a fire to warm frozen heart and long-chilled body.

"How many are there—of these Jacks?" Diskan asked Drustans.

"I do not know. They kept us prisoner on the ship. We saw only the guard and those with whom we have just been. Diskan"—his voice slowed—"do you not wonder how I came here?"

"As a prisoner, of course. Did you think I believed you one of them?"

A shadow of an expression Diskan could not read crossed the Vaan's face.

"I was stupid." Drustans' voice was sharp, almost as
182

if he resented Diskan's faith in him. "I believed a story concerning a need for verifying factors on a journey tape. So I took it, but it was not the one they wanted—"

"No. Because I had already stolen that," Diskan returned. He wanted to laugh, to shout, to run. What did it matter, all that which had happened on another world, in another time, to another person? The bubbling in him was something such as he had never known in all his drab days of life. This, this was freedom! It no longer mattered that he was big, clumsy, slow-witted—all those other inferiorities he had hugged to him. Yes, he had treasured his faults, using them to wall off a world he feared. He had no envy of Drustans now. He simply did not care about the Vaan or the life he represented any more.

"They tricked you, but I did it on my own," he said now. "I stole a tape, and a ship—which is now at the bottom of a bog hole. I'm probably certified 'unreliable'—"

"But we can question any such judgment!" Drustans broke in. "You will have a hearing, a chance for defense. Present circumstances will be in your favor—"

"A hearing if and when we get off this world," Diskan pointed out dryly.

"Help is coming; they knew that." Drustans spoke with his old confidence. "That's why Cincred was pushing so fast. The Patrol is hunting him. He had to scoop up any treasure and get off Mimir as quickly as he could. Once he spaced, he believed they could not trace him. Or, if by some chance they did, the authorities could not really prove anything. He could unload the loot with contacts not too far away. There would be plenty of suspicion, yes, but no illegal act could be brought home to him."

"They can get him now—they'll have witnesses."

"And when we get back to the spacer, I can set a beam call to bring in the Patrol cruiser!" Drustans began to trot.

It sounded very simple and quite easy. But surely

this Veep Cincred would not have left the ship without a guard, and Diskan mentioned that.

"True. But still we have a better chance now than we had even one time-unit ago. And perhaps—"

"Perhaps the Veep and the Jacks are still sniping at each other, yes. Only there are others to consider—"

"The natives?"

"No. Two survivors of the archaeological expedition."

They had reached the space below the steps. Diskan leaped, caught hold of the platform edge, and scrambled up and over. Drustans, the stiffness of the stass hold gone, pulled up beside him.

Brother, the hunt begins behind you.

Diskan was on his feet to look back. Nothing stirred down the city streets, but he did not doubt the truth of that warning. Either the Jacks or the Veep were there, if not in sight.

"We're being trailed now—"

Drustans spun around, intent upon the ruins. "I do not see them!"

But before the words were fairly out of his mouth, they did see a flash of blaster fire, cutting along a wall, leaving a glowing track on the aged stone. Not aimed at them but still on the trail they had just traversed.

Diskan made a decision. He caught the Vaan's upper arm.

"There's a badly wounded Zacathan here, and a girl. I haven't the training to operate a ship's com and you have. Will you try for the ship while I attempt to aid those others? If there is going to be any ray battle up this slope, they can well be caught in it!"

"What if we all go together?"

"No. You can move faster alone, and you know the ship. Wait—Julha has the stunner. That isn't much defense against a blaster, but it *is* a weapon and you won't have to go up against any ship guard bare-handed."

Diskan was already on the way, taking the steps in great strides, searching ahead for the point at which
184

he must cut off to find the crevice. The moonlight was so clear that he could almost have been walking in the brilliance of midday. Here—this was it!

"Julha!" He dared to call, not wanting to walk into a stunner beam. There—that was the opening to the crevice. A hiss from the shadows, then a whine—the furred one! It knew him, was welcoming—

Diskan and the Vaan crowded into that pocket so well protected by rock walls. Julha stood before the bundle that was Zimgrald. She looked at Diskan and then, beyond him, to Drustans, and her expression was one of vast relief.

"You have found help—" She swayed forward, but Diskan caught at her wrist, twisted the weapon from her loosening grasp, and thrust it at Drustans.

"Get going!" he ordered the Vaan. "And—"

Can you protect this one, see that he safely reaches the ship? He asked it of those others.

This is asking what is not of our concern, this meddling in the affairs of those who are not brothers. It was a silent protest.

It cannot then be done? Diskan's disappointment was acute.

Silence; then the faint impression of a conference he did not share in.

This is a thing that must be done for the good of that which lives in Xcothal?

This is a thing as right as thal patterns! Shall I swear it to you?

No need. Send this one who has no ears to hear the truth, no eyes to see. We shall take a part in this game, but you know the price.

Does one talk of price when one reaches for one's heart's desire? was Diskan's swift reply. Then he spoke aloud:

"You are going to have company, Drustans. How much they can or will do for you, I don't know. But they will aid as much as they are able."

Both the Vaan and Julha were eying him strangely. Drustans spoke first:

"The natives?"

Diskan nodded and dropped one hand to rest it for a moment on the head near his thigh. "The brothers-in-fur. Now go!"

Julha protested, but the Vaan was already on his way, the stunner in his hand, the furred one streaking to pass him.

"Where is he going? What do you do now?" She caught at Diskan and tried to draw him away as he stooped over the Zacathan.

"In a very little while," Diskan told her, "they are going to come out of Xcothal fighting. And I don't fancy being caught in any blaster crossfire. We move, back toward the ship, and Drustans is already on his way to get help—"

"Our people have returned? But they would come at once for Zimgrald! Didn't you tell them he is here? No, you can't move him!"

"I can and will. The only ship now planeted is a Jack one. There is a chance, a slim one, that Drustans can get on board that and signal in a Patrol cruiser he believes is trailing these Jacks. Now, don't ask any more questions—get going!"

Diskan spoke harshly with a purpose. She snatched some things from their packs while he picked up the Zacathan, grunting as he stood under the alien's weight. With the girl before him, Diskan came out of the crevice and started the climb to the old road.

Shadows flowed about the rocks, but he had no fear of those, saying quickly to the girl:

"Don't be frightened. The furred ones are with us. They will give any alarm." The limp body he carried was heavy, but this night he felt as if he could do anything, that he now possessed all the strength and energy in the world!

They wound among the rocks to the crest of the ridge.

"Back in the city," Julha cried out. "That was a blaster. Who are they fighting? Our people—Mik?"

"Each other," Diskan replied briefly.

186

"Why?"

"Because they discovered what they were hunting—"

"The treasure! Oh, no!" She was distressed. "The High One, the finding should have been his—"

"They found *their* treasure," Diskan corrected. "It was what they wanted of Xcothal. I believe that Zimgrald sought something else here. Xcothal has more than one treasure to offer—"

It had—it had! He held that knowledge to him to warm, to strengthen, to arm him against anything that might come out of the night to try him now.

And he was not really aware of the passing of time until the girl stumbled and fell, and he was alerted to that by the furred ones.

"I cannot go on," Julha told him in a small voice. "Do you, and I shall catch up."

"There is no need. For the time, we are safe. Here—"

It was another rock pocket, but it did not face the marsh and the city; rather it faced that distant valley where the ship stood. The watchers were all about them in a protecting screen. Julha knelt by the Zacathan, her hands touching the beak-nosed face of the tranced man tenderly.

"He still lives and sleeps," she said.

"And while he lives, there is hope." Diskan repeated her own earlier words.

"Please, what happened? Did you find the cache, and who is that man who came with you?"

Diskan cut the story to its bare framework, but when he came to the scene in the wedge chamber, when he had wrought the treasure of Xcothal for those determined to have it, Diskan hesitated. Who would believe unless they had seen, unless they had done as he had? Was all that, too, only an illusion? But *he* knew it was not! Only he could not tell that part of the story. It lay too close to the secret of his own treasure, which was not to be shared, could not be shared.

"They thought they had found what they sought," he told her.

"Part of the illusion." She nodded, and since she had made that a statement instead of a question, Diskan need only keep silence.

"And that set them at one another," he continued, giving her the rest of it as it had happened.

"Then"—her hand went out to smooth the covers about the Zacathan—"they did not really discover anything at all! It is still waiting for the High One. When this is over, he can take up his search!"

Diskan tensed. More prying, more delving—to break open the heart of Xcothal?

Not so, brother. To those who have no eyes, no ears, there is neither sight nor sound nor being. Perhaps later there may come those who have the sight and hearing—and to those Xcothal will open a door, many doors. But to others—nothing. And they will tire of their fruitless searching and go, ceasing to seek what may not be found—by them. The swift, wordless answer came.

"Perhaps he may," Diskan agreed, but he thought that Zimgrald—even if he survived his hurt—might never return to Xcothal.

"And if he does," he continued, "you will aid him?"

Her hands moved as if she were shoving away some burden she could not bring herself to assume again. "If he asks—I will. But—"

"But you hope he will not ask—that is the truth of it? Do you hate the city so?"

"I—I think I fear it. Something slumbers there. To wake it—"

"Would change a world!" Diskan said softly.

"But I do not want that change!" she whispered.

"Then for you it will not come. Do not fear; it will not come—"

She raised her eyes. "You—you are different. And you know something, do you not?"

Diskan nodded. "I know something. I have seen the world change—"

"And you were not afraid." Again it was a statement, not a question.

188

"Yes, in a manner I was afraid, very much afraid."

"But you are not now."

"No."

Brother—from the sky—it comes!

Diskan could see it, too, a star with no fixed position, making a fiery sweep across the sky. That was a ship, orbiting in, near to tailing down. The Patrol?

"A ship!" Julha had seen it now and was on her feet. "Help for us?"

"I think so—can you go on now?"

"Yes, oh, yes!"

Diskan took up the burden of the Zacathan. Now that it was so near the end, he was plagued by last wisps of doubt. What he was going to do was to close a door firmly, and once closed, that portal could not be opened again. In spite of the sorrows of the past, it was hard to make so radical a change in the future.

Julha was half running, half trotting, but Diskan's pace was far slower. This could be the last walk he would ever take with his own kind.

One comes!

"Diskan?" A call out of the night.

"Drustans—here!" That call had come from some distance away, giving him a few more moments.

He put down Zimgrald. Perhaps of them all, the Zacathan could come the closest to understanding this—a twist of the X factor no man could control once it entered his life. But still there were those last-minute doubts, a feeling of being pulled in two directions, until he lost some of the brave certainty that had filled him most of this night.

"Why are you waiting here?" Julha came running back. "The High One—is he worse?" She threw herself on her knees beside Zimgrald, her hands busy about his wrapped body.

"He is the same—"

Perhaps some tone of Diskan's voice drew attention away from the alien. Diskan was peeling off the parka, then unbuckling his belt, dropping them both beside the recumbent form of the Zacathan.

189

"What—what are you doing?"

"I am going. You are safe. Drustans will be here very soon. The Patrol ship is planeting—"

"You mean—because you are an outlaw, you are afraid they will force you into rehabilitation? But they can't—they won't, not after we tell them all you have done here! We shall testify for you!"

Diskan laughed. He had almost forgotten that he must be judged a criminal—unreliable, subject to punishment by his kind or by *her* kind. He had moved too far down another road.

"I am not afraid of the Patrol," he said, still amused. "No, Julha, I am returning to Xcothal because that is now my world—"

"But what you saw there is all illusion!" she cried. "An empty ruin is what it really is. You will die there of cold and hunger."

"Perhaps"—one of his doubts came to the surface— "perhaps you are right and I am walking into an hallucination or dream. But it is mine, far more mine than this world of yours in which I now stand. I am going back, perhaps, as you say, to die among broken ruins and tumbled stones. But to me Xcothal is not dead—it lives and in it thal runs, sweet waters flow, there are things that can be shaped by the mind as your world shapes them by hands. And there are those who await me there with a welcome I have never known in your world—"

"You can't! You'll be rayed by the Jacks—" She gave another argument.

Diskan shook his head. In spite of the cold, he was fumbling with the catches of his tunic, pulling off the garment that had always seemed too confining to his big arms and wide shoulders.

"I will not enter *their* Xcothal." He dropped the tunic. "Good voyaging, Julha. When the High One recovers, tell him he was very right. The furred ones—they are the key if one can use them. And there is a treasure in Xcothal that surpasses all the wealth of the worlds beyond. Tell him I have proved it!"

"No!" She tried to catch him as he turned. But then he was running among the rocks, paying no heed to his footing even in the rough country, not aware of the cold about his bare upper body. And around him bounded in plain sight the furred ones, leaping and playfully springing upon one another in their exuberance.

In time, Diskan came to the stair and descended it with great strides. Then he stood on the platform, impatiently tearing from him the last bits of clothing that were of the past, the last ties with what had been.

Before him was a straight running stream of water, sweet water, which was the road, and through that moved the shadows. But these were shadows no longer, for he saw them at last for what they were—bodies like his own—not aliens—though even with different shaping they could not be strange. And in their eyes recognition, welcome for the unlocker of doors, the one uniting brothers-in-fur with brothers-in-flesh—who might lead also to the surmounting of still farther and stranger barriers—

And with a shout of greeting, Diskan leaped forward, into the sweet water, the color, the life that was Xcothal, the Xcothal that had been and now was again!

Let COVENTRY Give You
A Little Old-Fashioned Romance

☐ **PERDITA**   50173 $1.95
    by Joan Smith

☐ **QUADRILLE**   50174 $1.95
    by Marion Chesney

☐ **HEIR TO ROWANLEA**   50175 $1.95
    by Sally James

☐ **PENNY WISE**   50176 $1.95
    by Sarah Carlisle

☐ **THE TANGLED WEB**   50177 $1.95
    by Barbara Hazard

☐ **MISS MOUSE**   50178 $1.95
    by Mira Stables

Buy them at your local bookstore or use this handy coupon for ordering.

COLUMBIA BOOK SERVICE (a CBS Publications Co.)
32275 Mally Road, P.O. Box FB, Madison Heights, MI 48071

Please send me the books I have checked above. Orders for less than 5 books must include 75¢ for the first book and 25¢ for each additional book to cover postage and handling. Orders for 5 books or more postage is FREE. Send check or money order only.

Cost $_____   Name _____

Sales tax*_____   Address _____

Postage_____   City _____

Total $_____   State _____ Zip _____

The government requires us to collect sales tax in all states except AK, DE, MT, NH and OR.

This offer expires 1 January 82   8153